Can't We Ever Go Home?

Can't We Ever Go Home?

by Barbara Rowland Lubick

to Rolf (aka Owl, owl),
a good friend.
whom I've enjoyed knowing.
Best Wishes,
Barbara

I have tried to recreate events, locales and conversations based on stories and memories of my mother, Celia Heuer Bloom. In some instances I have changed the names of individuals and places, I may have changed some identifying characteristics. Certain details are imagined. Certain occurrences are purely fiction. It is my hope that the benevolent spirit of the Jewish Orphan's Home is maintained.

ISBN: 1514763206
ISBN 13: 9781514763209
Library of Congress Control Number: 2015910966
CreateSpace Independent Publishing Platform, North Charleston, SC

Dedicated to

Lauren Elaine
Joseph David
Richard Arthur Dan
Morry

Acknowledgments

Illustration by
Lauren Rowland and Richard Rowland

Photographs by
Seaver Center for Western History Research,
Los Angeles County Museum of Natural History

Edited by
Richard Rowland
Aaron Fischer
Louis Bloom
and special thanks to Toni Lopopolo

Special Thanks to
Craig Hornung
Vista Del Mar Child and Family Services
Jewish Orphan's Home records

Thanks to Judy Flowers for providing Julius Raphael's memoir

Thanks to Joseph Rowland for his corroboration and support

Book Design by
Lauren Rowland

Contents

Chapter 1

Leaving New York

The new high school near my house is scheduled to open this fall, 1916, but I don't want to go to this Thomas Jefferson High, even if it is modeled after Monticello and is supposed to be so modern. It's dark outside now, so I can't really see its outline behind the low houses down the block.

I'm standing on a nearby corner and warm breezes are swirling my skirt around my legs. I hear the streetcar clanging from down the street. A branch from the avocado tree in the yard behind me bends low and messes up some strands of my hair. This warm evening has turned even darker now, but I can still make out the metal grill on the front of the number 9 streetcar as it clatters closer.

I press my hand over my skirt pocket to feel the coins. Yes, there is enough money for me to take the streetcar. I know the way. I could step right up onto the streetcar when it stops at the cement island in front of me and head back to the Orphans' Home. I can finish the term with my class, participate in the performance I've rehearsed, see my friends.

But I'm not an orphan.

And I was not back when our voyage to California began.

Why my papa wanted to take us far away to California, I don't know. I was happy here in the Bronx, in the neighborhood where I was born. But I was only seven then, so what could I know about decisions that grown-ups make.

I loved the Bronx. I loved playing on the cobblestones in the courtyard with my cousins. Even when my cousin Isaac teased me and ran off to hide I loved it there. I didn't mind when he popped out from the old horse stalls to pretend to scare me.

I just laughed. All the kids laughed. We played and laughed together every day.

Why Papa wanted to move again after coming so far from where he was born in Europe I couldn't understand.

"Will I have to go to a new school?" I whispered to Mama. She tucked me in for the night and said, "Shh."

I slept in the bed next to my little sister Bella. But she was fast asleep and couldn't hear Mama whisper back,

"Of course. What else? You think you can come back to New York all the way from California to go to your old school?" She smiled, plumped up my pillow.

I turned over to face the wall. I wished she wouldn't make me feel dumb.

I loved my school as much as the courtyard. I went to sleep thinking about how I'd miss my class.

We went to school in long buildings and we opened the partitions between classrooms so all the different grades could say the pledge of allegiance together. Getting together made us feel so proud and patriotic. Plus, I was a good student and brought home good notices to Mama and Papa.

But the move wasn't up to me. Papa got the notion that if we moved to California—an exotic and faraway place—Mama's health would improve and we would make a better living.

So before any of us knew it we packed our huge green trunk with all our clothes. I helped Mama wrap the dishes in old newspapers. Bella tried to help, but she just crumpled up her sheets of paper, so I pushed her hands away. She was too young. "Wait till you're five," I told her. She smiled and made more balls out of paper, lined them up on the floor.

It made me feel grown-up to help, but I still wasn't happy about packing.

Our room upstairs was bare now, except for the trunk in the middle of the room.

Bella tried to open the lid to stuff in her scruffy rag doll. I yanked it out of her hand. "You can't take that."

"Yes, I can. It's my baby."

"Papa will buy you a new doll, a clean one. You'll see."

"I don't want a new one." She scrambled to reach the doll, and fell against the side of the trunk. She slid down on her bottom and cried.

"Here. Take it." I tossed it to her. Her tears stopped the minute she got it back.

"Baby," she mumbled, and rocked the shabby doll in her arms. She looked up at me from the corner of her eye.

"Aren't you scared?" she asked. Her thick black hair was cut in a short bob. It moved with her head like it was pasted on in a chunk. My hair was light in color and wispy thin, not thick like my sister's. Sometimes I wore it in two long braids so it wouldn't blow away.

She set her doll down on the floor, looked me in the eye. "Scared to go so far I mean?"

"No. We have to. Papa said so. I'm not scared, but I'd still rather stay here."

"Uncle Jacob said there'd be wild Indians there."

"I guess Papa doesn't think so."

She went back to rocking her baby.

I heard Sam's voice in the hall along with some scrapes and bangs. He's our oldest brother. He knows a lot. I ran to the door, shouted back to Bella, "I'll go ask Sam."

For the last few days our brothers, Sam, who was almost twelve years old, and Abe, who was ten, helped with moving the heavy furniture down the stairs to our neighbors' houses.

I ran down the narrow stairs after Sam and grabbed on to his sleeve. He set down the chair he carried. "What?"

"We really have to go, don't we?"

He picked the chair up again. "It's what Papa wants."

"Bella thinks there'll be wild Indians there."

"Naw. California's just orange trees and sun. So they say." He tossed his head and rolled his eyes. "Bella's only four. She'll believe anything. Tell her about the orange trees."

He shifted the chair in his arms and clunked on down the stairs. His high top boots thumped against the chair legs, loud at first then softer the farther he went.

I didn't think he wanted to move either, but he didn't complain, at least that I could hear. It was hard to know what he was thinking because my brothers were always gone, selling newspapers or helping on the produce carts of my uncles and father. I mostly saw them at supper time, when they slurped their soup and pulled so much bread off our loaf.

Once Sam took a piece of roast beef off Abe's plate and Papa reached over and smacked him on the head. But Abie never cared about what Sam did, because he was so generous and sweet.

Papa insisted that we should look nice for the trip and that we should be prepared to arrive in the land of milk and honey, ready for any event. I remember Mama shook her head in disbelief when he took us girls to the shop where his friend sold raincoats.

She said, "Louis, what do they need those for? Rain never falls in California."

He didn't answer her, but told us, "Pick out the ones you like, *maidlach*, girls." I had my eye on a red one with white piping around the hood. But right away Mama strode over to the rack and picked out two blue plaid ones. My heart sank.

"Hold on." Papa went over to her and took hold of the smaller one by the hanger. "That can be for Bella. Do you like it, Bellie?"

She felt the slippery material with her fingers and nodded.

"Which one do you want, Celie?"

Papa seemed to know what I'd been thinking. I pointed to the one I liked. Mama picked it up and measured it against my body. I held my breath.

"It will do. Big enough to grow into."

Papa paid for the raincoats and we walked home to finish packing.

So many of our relatives crowded around us at the train station to say goodbye the day we started our journey. Mama and her sisters hugged each other and cried. Papa told them, "This is just the beginning. You will all come to California, one by one, and we will all live the same way we do now. Wait and see. I'll pave the way."

They nodded, and my cousin Isaac, hiding behind my aunt's long skirts, kicked me to let me know he didn't want to come later. I wanted to kick him back, but it was time to board the train.

At first I was excited to look out the window to see all the buildings and then farms and cows. But that became boring fast, and uncomfortable. I stood up. Mama took hold of the back of my dress at the neck and sat me back down. "How come Sam and Abie don't have to stay in their seats?" It was clear that my older brothers were allowed to go walking, balancing back and forth through the aisles of train cars but Bella and I had to sit.

From the seat behind me Papa's voice came through. "Do what Mama says."

Bella made a face at me. I turned away. She had to sit as still as I did.

Finally, after what seemed like a week, but was only a few days, we came to the stop in Albuquerque. I was the first one to look out the window and see the wild Indians.

"Look!" I screamed. "They're real!" One, in a huge feathered headdress put his nose right up to our window. Bella screamed. She clung to Papa. He told her, "Dolly, they're just pretending."

Sam came over and looked out the window from behind us. "They're real, all right. But they're not wild."

Papa said, "They're down to selling handmade baskets and jewelry. But they dress up fancy, the better to sell their goods. See?"

We were allowed to get down off the platform. I watched an Indian woman who had a multi-colored blanket wrapped around her head and shoulders. She was feeding her baby who was tucked inside. I must have followed her, because when I looked up, I was lost among unfamiliar faces milling about.

I stood still, not knowing where to go. The passengers who'd gotten off to stretch their legs blocked any view I might have had of my family.

Maybe my parents would get back on the train and go on without me. At first I was too scared to even cry. Then when I heard the engine whistle my tears just burst out.

Crowds were now all going in the same direction. Maybe I should follow. But what if I'd miss them? I stood still, afraid to move.

The whistle blew again and smoke from the engine filled the air, making me cough through my tears. I wiped my eyes with my sleeve. This dress would have to last for my whole trip, but now I didn't care if it got dirty.

Off in the distance, above the heads of all those hurrying men and women were the tallest mountains I'd ever seen. Through my tears I watched white clouds floating above them.

Soft as a cloud was a sudden touch on my arm.

Sam! They'd sent him to find me. I should have known. I tried not to show him my teary face. He took me by the hand and led me back to Mama. Sam was the oldest boy and I was the oldest girl, so we often were paired off. I felt he understood me the best. He knew what I went through when I started school, because he'd been the first in our family to attend school.

Abraham, who we all called Abie, or sometimes just Abe, was Bella's special brother. He paired off with her because he understood what it was like to be the younger one. They were the two babies—told too often that they were too young.

When we got back on the train, Papa presented me with a little turquoise ring he'd bought from one of the squaws. Mama pushed herself in as he placed it on my finger.

"See?" she said. I let him buy it for you."

I looked up at her, questioning.

"Mama understood," Papa told me. "She could see those folks are even poorer than we are."

She smiled at me, patted me on the hand, over the ring.

Papa turned to Mama, "I gave Abe some coins to buy a tomahawk." He whispered to us. "He was staring at it through the window."

He reached across to the seat in front of us. "Let's see your tomahawk, Abe."

Abe turned back toward us, a funny little grin on his face.

"I didn't buy it, Papa. I bought a little papoose doll for Bella instead."

I watched while the whole family admired the doll in its wrapper of fawn skin, feathers and beads.

"That's a real cute doll, Bella." I cuddled closer to her on our seat.

"You can play with me if you want."

"Thanks."

"I didn't like it when you were lost," she whispered.

I kissed the top of her head.

When we reached Los Angeles it was clear to me, even though I was just a kid, that Mama felt awfully sad about how our hotel looked. The room where we all had to sleep was drafty and the wood floors were cold and they creaked. Worst of all, it did rain. Mama had to tell Papa he was right when he unpacked our raincoats. But we mostly stayed inside because the streets outside were all muddy. Sam and Abe got to go out with Papa.

I stared out the window for those few days and called Bella over whenever a few rays of sun showed between the steady raindrops.

Just when Mama told Papa she wanted to go back home, somehow our family got to buy a house in the south part of Los Angeles. What a relief that was. At least for Mama. I secretly hoped we might have to go back to New York.

I heard Mama tell the new neighbors that it rained for two weeks when we got into town. I don't think it was really that long a time, but it sure seemed like it, stuck inside in a cold room as we were.

I'll never know how he did it, but Papa got us a wonderful house with a big, open yard. Right away he got us a new horse. We named him Blackie like our old horse even though he was white because we all agreed, Blackie is such a nice name for a horse. Nice Blackie had a little shed to stay in, open on three sides. "Papa, how come there's no barn like I thought farms have?" I asked, because all my books showed big red barns with haystacks. He answered, "We don't need a barn. Didn't your mama say it never rained in California?"

What?! "Yes, Papa," I said, but I was really puzzled. Then he laughed so I knew he made a joke.

But our new place really was like a little farm. In New York our stables only had dark, narrow stalls for our horses that pulled the vegetable carts—no room for chickens or other animals like we had now.

We got a goat, Butsy, and we had lots of chickens and best of all, we had a big orange tree that gave us delicious, juicy oranges. Mama was so proud of our farm she made Papa hire a photographer to show us in the yard with all the animals. She put on a sunbonnet and an apron, and held the pan to throw the chicken feed on the ground. This was to show all our aunts and uncles and my grandma and our cousins. Maybe they would think California was great and decide to move out here faster.

I loved Butsy. But only after I got over being afraid of her. Bella took longer not to feel scared. One day Mama cut up some carrots in the kitchen. She handed them to me and sent me out the back door. "Take these to feed to the horse," she said.

I went outside, stepped with care to avoid the chicken messes. Bella came up and, instead of taking the carrot pieces to the horse, I got a better idea.

"Take these to Butsy," I said. "She'll love you for it. Hold them out one by one. And be careful not to let your fingers get too close to her mouth."

She took them, but only because she wanted to show me she wasn't really afraid.

"Here, Butsy," we both coaxed.

Butsy didn't need much coaxing. She came running toward Bella in a fast charge. Bella had her hand out with one of the pieces ready for Butsy to take, but this was too much for her. She threw all the carrots at the charging animal and ran away fast.

I looked down while Butsy gulped the pieces in huge mouthfuls, and I would not look up because I didn't want Bella to see how hard I was holding back laughing out loud.

The sun way up high over our yard felt nice the way it warmed my arms. It made the oranges that hung from the leafy branches of our trees glisten. It even shone on Bella's short black hair so it shined, too.

The courtyard where I loved to play back home never looked so bright, but I never cared about that. Dark and all, it felt like my real home.

Chapter 2

Celia Enrolled in School in California, Eucalyptus Pods

Mama and Papa enrolled all four of us kids in the neighborhood school right away. Even Bella got to go, because kindergarten started earlier in California than in the Bronx. My school back in New York must have been way ahead. I'd learned so much, they skipped me up to fourth grade.

From my desk at the back I admired all the colorful book reports that they had pinned up along the wall. I smiled at the teacher.

She'd seemed nice when I first came in, but now she acted strict. She said harshly, "Sit up here, Celia. Front row, please."

Then she turned back to face the blackboard. Her black dress matched the blackboard and only her collar stood out white beneath her dark, upswept hair. Her smile had been kind but when she wheeled around so fast it felt cold.

I knew the children at their desks must be looking at me as I made my way along the aisle by the wall. I kept my eyes on their drawings pinned up next to their papers marked with red As and Bs.

I lowered my head and wondered if maybe I'd been squinting and that's how the teacher figured out that I couldn't see the board very well. Or maybe she made me move because I was shorter than the older kids.

The playground here was bigger than ours back home. Leafy trees lined the edges of the play area. Scattered benches looked inviting.

At recess I stood still under the shadiest tree. I hoped the other girls would let me play with them and I'd make new friends. But no one invited me to jump rope or swing or kick the ball. The girls in my class played together and didn't pay attention to me, or ask me my name or anything

After a while I noticed a small crowd of girls gathered under the farthest tree. I told myself that I had to make the first move to make friends. That's what Mama said anyway. I tightened my hands into fists, took a breath and walked up to this crowd of tall girls in gathered full skirts and long sleeved blouses, their elbows all touching each other. I couldn't think what to say, but stood there, forcing a little smile.

The tallest girl turned around, faced me, and said. "Listen. We're telling secrets. You're too young." She swished her skirts back. The girl next to her looked at me with pity in her eyes. "When you're older you'll understand. See?"

Another girl looked at me sideways. "It's about boys. Get it?"

"I have brothers. I know about boys," I mumbled.

A thin, dark-haired girl opened her mouth to say something, then shrugged. "Wait till you're older, okay?"

"Sure." I went back to the bench closest to the bungalow where the door to my new class stood open, waited for the bell to ring, held my arms tight in front of my chest.

At home I had no one my age to play with. Bella ran around the neighborhood and found a little girl named Gracie. They had a good time because Bella and Gracie were the same size and the same age. They played outside all the time. Jump rope, hopscotch, everything.

I wouldn't have minded if my cousin Isaac from New York would move out here. He could be rough and he sometimes teased me, but he also knew games we liked to play together.

I thought I might find some kids my own age if I walked in the other direction from school. Maybe toward the railroad tracks, where

I wasn't supposed to go by myself. It would be okay, just for today.

I started off down the street, ducked my head to avoid the low branches of a banana tree. Then a horse and buggy clip-clopped down the cross street and blocked my view. I tried peering around, up and down. No one was in sight. It was getting late. Maybe I'd try again another day.

Well, that was okay. I'd rather read, anyway.

Most of the time now I stayed inside alone and read books about fairy tales. I loved the stories about princes answering riddles and rescuing lovely princesses.

"Celia!" Mama shouted. "Go out and play. Not good for you to stay in the house all the time." She shook my shoulder as I lay on the bed, my face in my book. I couldn't push my own mama away and keep reading. I got up, set my open book face down on the bed, and wandered into the living room.

I heard the sounds of jumping feet, swishes of clothes and giggles coming from outside. I looked out the window and saw Bella toss her jump rope to Gracie. Gracie caught it by the handle. She tied one end of her long rope to a tree trunk. She ran farther back onto the sidewalk, twirled the rope in a high arc then low. Bella jumped in and they sang out together, "Engine, engine, number nine. Going down the Chicago line."

Oh, good. They'll need me to hold the other end.

I ran down the steps and out toward the tree to untie that end. But Bella came toward me and pulled on my hand.

"Jump in with me. We'll jump together."

I tripped in. The rope got tangled in my feet. Gracie stopped twirling. She untied the rope from the tree herself. "You can jump later. It's my turn now." She frowned at me as she held the untied end out to me. "Are you sure you can turn it?"

"Sure I can. But put it back around the tree, because I have to go in now."

Bella stared at me. She didn't say come back or anything.

They would have let me keep playing, but I didn't want them to see me in case I tripped again. Besides, I had a better idea. I walked through the kitchen and out the back door. The wooden steps down from the porch creaked as I jumped from one to the other on down to the ground. Mama's clothesline was sagging low. She hadn't hung any clothes on it today. I pulled until it loosened from the wooden posts on each end and plopped down. I tied one end to a tree in the back yard, just like I saw Bella doing in the front. Then I tried to twirl the other end and jump in. Impossible. I kept tripping.

"Celia! What are you doing?!" Mama rushed out the back door. She wiped her hands on her apron and ran toward me. I dropped the rope on the ground.

"Now look. You got it dirtier." She picked it up and brushed at it with her hand to get the dust off.

"I didn't mean to, Mama." I tried brushing at a part of the clothesline, but she snatched it away to tie it back up on the posts.

I left her there, fastening it up, and went back in my bedroom. I had to see how the prince solved that riddle. How would he save the princess? Swim across the moat? Shoot his bow and arrow into the forest? I didn't worry that Mama would tell Papa what I did with the rope, because he never got mad at me.

I hated it here, and I wanted to tell Papa that. But I couldn't because he seemed so happy.

Mama wrote letters to her sisters and brothers back home in New York. She missed her family so much, and the mail took ages for answers to come. Papa worked on his wagon peddling produce all day, so Mama had to find things to do with her day. I thought maybe she could ask papa to take us back to New York.

I sat on the front porch after school. The orange peels I'd thrown into the bushes smelled real strong, not sweet like the blossoms in the trees.

Mama came walking fast up the sidewalk

I spit out some seeds, wiped my mouth and stood up. "What did you buy, Mama?"

She opened her bags and showed me some papers. "I found out about a night class at the high school. It's to make better my

English." She hugged me. "So I'm starting school, too. Wait till I tell the family." She pushed open the screen door. I sat back down on a step.

Now what. She'll never tell Papa to go back. There's nobody I can tell that I hate it here. I put my head down in my hands.

Our new house sat pretty close to the railroad tracks on the east side of Central Avenue. We'd settled south of downtown Los Angeles where Papa could go straight from our street to the central market to pick up his produce. We had to walk past some fields to get to the railroad tracks on the other side.

Weeds and low bushes grew in sparse patches all along the track. Towering over them in a long row grew tall, huge eucalyptus trees.

"Come walk with me, girls. Take one of these bags." Mama handed us each a cloth bag with string handles.

At the tracks Bella and I balanced on a rail, stretched out our arms, pretended we were tightrope-walking.

"Get off of there, girls. A train might come."

"Okay." I knew she'd say that. I was about to fall off anyway.

The birds sang in the trees, small gusts of warm wind blew the leaves around. I stepped between tall shadows on the dry earth.

Mama walked with care, avoided stones and pieces of bark. "See these trees, girls? So different than our tress back home. Tall and straight up in the air. Such drooping, yellow leaves. And look, you should look on the ground."

Between brown leaves and broken twigs I could see little round pods, shaped like starfish in tiny helmets. I picked one up. The pod felt hard and rough.

"Fill your bags, girls. I need a lot."

"What do you want these for, anyhow?" I held up a pod.

"You'll see." Mama wandered farther away where she saw more leaves and pods fallen in heaps. I followed along.

We heard a faint whistle from the train. Mama and I turned back to look.

The whistle blew louder, and we spotted Bella standing on a rail, her leg twisted, her boot stuck inside.

My head turned toward her, my eyes stared. My body froze into a statue.

Mama dropped her bag, screamed and ran. When she reached out to grab her, Bella jumped away from the track onto the ground, and the train whizzed by with a loud swoosh. .

Mama hugged and shook and spanked and yelled at Bella all the same time. .

I stood there and shook. My body wouldn't come to life. I hated myself. I wanted to run to Bella and grab her myself, but I hadn't moved. Yet, I knew that in one more minute, if Mama hadn't got there first, I am SURE I would have unfrozen and ran to Bella myself to rescue her. That's what I thought. Yes, I was sure of it.

"But, Mama," Bella insisted. "I wasn't stuck. I was waiting to see the train."

Mama smacked her again on her bottom. Then she hugged her again. She let go of her and leaned against a tree.

I managed to walk up to Mama. "She's okay. I'll get your bag for you. Rest here, Mama."

I picked up a few more pods, stuffed them in her bag and put a few more in mine.

Mama took hold of each of us girls by the hand and we headed toward home. First we had to cross those awful tracks to get back to our house. I whispered, "I hate you, tracks, I hate you, railroads, I hate you, trains."

"What did you say?" Bella asked.

"Be quiet," I told her. How could I say what I was feeling? That if anything happened to my little sister I could never breathe again. In fact, I was still shaking inside.

Mama didn't say anything all the way back. Maybe she was thinking like I was—that trains in New York aren't so much out in the open where little kids can get suck on them like here in dumb old California.

While we were at school the next week Mama took a needle and some strong string. She threaded the pods in rows. On Saturday she asked us to help her.

"Ouch!" The needle stuck my finger. With my hurt finger in my mouth I mumbled, "Those pods are hard, Mama."

"My needle bent before it went through." Bella held up her bent needle and laughed at how crazy it looked.

"Use a stone," Mama told us. "See? If you push it with the stone it goes right through."

I went outside and picked up some hard rocks from our yard to bring back in so we could string the pods easier. We helped Mama make lots of these long strings.

When she felt we had enough she hung them side by side in the fronts of our closets that had no doors. We couldn't afford the glass beads that were all the style for closet covers in those days. Besides, the pods smelled good, and made our clothes smell good.

I sniffed my clothes when I was getting dressed for school in the morning. "Bella, you know? It was worth that work stringing these. Smell your dress."

She came over to the closet, rummaged through all the clothes, even our brothers' extra shirts, putting her nose to them all." "Uhm, hum. You're right."

I hugged her. She grinned at me. It was so nice when we agreed about things.

We'd been in our house almost a year when Papa came home with startling news. First he put Blackie in his shed, brushed and fed him, then came in and washed up for dinner. Abe and Sam secured the wagon. Abie was first to follow Papa inside. He started to wash up at the sink in our little bathroom.

I peeked in, saw Sam, taller than Abe, rush in, and push his brother aside. Abie stuck his hand in the sink and splashed water up onto Sam's dark curls. Sam scooped water onto Abie's lighter, straighter hair, and they would have had a play water fight but our mother knew the way to stop them. She called out, "Eat! It shouldn't get cold!"

We all sat down for our soup. Mama almost always started us out with big bowls of soup, thick with noodles or with delicious vegetables and floating crackers.

"Esther."

We kids looked up even though Papa looked straight at Mama.

"You want the relatives should come? This is a small house, right?"

"What are you getting at?" She said what we all were wondering.

"I found a house with an extra bedroom. And a back porch you can put a bed in."

"But Louis. Moving again? We like this house." She set down her spoon, took her fingers off the handle. "I like the neighbors."

"What about school?" Abraham asked what the rest of us didn't dare put into words. "I like this school."

"AHA! Papa stood up at the head of the table. The new house is only two blocks from here." Bella put her lips in a circle and made a whistling sound. I knew it was because she felt relieved, and I think we all knew why. She would still be able to run out and play with her friend Gracie.

At bedtime Bella knelt down alongside my bed, put her head close to mine on the pillow.

"Celia, are you really glad we can go to the same school when we move?"

"Yes." I tucked my nightgown under my legs. "Why?"

"Remember what you told me? And you said that you didn't want me to tell Mama or Papa? About those mean girls at school?" She put her lips next to my ear, said, "I never told them."

"Oh, Sweetie. That's all over now. I should have told you." I sat up in bed. Bella's nightie was pink with lace inserts where my blue nightie had lacier ones. I reached out and hugged her. Our nightgowns made a pretty pink and blue pattern across my blanket. "Bella, I found a nice bunch of girls. They make fun of those other girls, the ones who think they're so big. I have lots of friends at school now."

"You do? Since when?"

"When the new term started. I had a seat next to a real smart girl and we did our work together. Then we went out on the playground together, and all her friends made friends with me."

"That's good." Bella looked so solemn.

"Come on. Give me a kiss goodnight." I lay back down. "Next time your class is on the playground look for me. You'll see me with my friends. Okay?"

She nodded.

Now that Bella was six she understood so much more.

Chapter 3

The New House, Moving Day, Cousins

"Oh, Butsy. I love you so much." I wrapped my arms around the goat's neck. Her normal na na sound came out softer and lower than usual. I kissed her on the top of her head, behind her ear.

"Now, get away." Sam pushed my arms off. "Let me put this on." He slipped a rope over Butsy's neck.

He tugged. "Come on." He tried pulling her up the dirt path along the side of our house to the street. But she stood still. I kissed her again.

"I love her too." Bella ran over and kissed the goat on her scraggly side.

Abe pulled Bella away. "Sweetie, she knows you love her. Don't get your face dirty." He wiped her mouth with his handkerchief.

Sam jerked the rope, frowned, and said, "If you had to clean up her ka ka you wouldn't be sad that she has to go. Come on, Abe." Together, they led the goat away.

"I'll miss you, Butsy," I called after her.

Bella slipped her arm around my waist. We both made sad faces. I took both her hands in mine and made my face even sadder. My mouth turned down until I looked ridiculous, until we both saw how funny that was. We couldn't help laughing.

Bella wiped her eyes with the back of her hand. We couldn't hear Butsy any longer, but the birds were chirping and clanging noises came from the street. "Celia, you'll like it after we move," Bella said.

"I know. It's just that... Well, school's okay now. But.... Oh, Look. There's that man, the one Papa sold the goat to." I pointed to the end of our path to the sidewalk in front.

"Sold Butsy!" Bella, her fists firm on her waist, planted her feet far apart, her forehead a line of scowls.

"It's okay, Sweetie. He's going to a farm."

We walked together to the front of the house where the man Papa sold our goat to waited with his wagon. Crates with our chickens penned up inside waited on the wagon in stacks.

Sam handed the rope over, turned back to us.

"You okay, Girls?"

Abie nodded in the direction of the crates of chickens. "Mama won't mind not having to sweep up after those fellows."

I sniffed. "But we won't have the eggs."

"We can buy eggs cheap," Abie said.

"Yes, Celia. We can buy eggs cheap." Bella thought that whatever her brother Abie said was so good she had to repeat it.

"Sure, Abraham." I used his full name when I was making my point. "Mama didn't like collecting those eggs that much anyway."

Butsy baa'd on her way up the ramp onto the truck.

I'd seen enough. I ran back to the yard behind the house and clomped up the creaky back stairs into the house.

The rooms looked empty with our furniture missing. Mama had bundled our clothes to go last. The cloth bundles stood in rows along the hall. Mostly they were tied up neatly, but a few lumps and bumps sticking out at their sides gave them an air of waiting impatiently.

Papa finished with the man outside, then rushed into the living room. He banged the door so hard we heard it clang against the frame. He wore his good black pants and a clean white shirt with the sleeves rolled up. His black hair and black mustache made such a contrast with the white shirt that when he filled the door frame he looked like a photograph to me. I loved how my Papa looked.

"Celia, are you ready? Where's Mama?" He patted me on the head. He hurried into the kitchen without waiting for me to answer him.

"Esther. We have to go now." I almost covered my ears because his voice boomed so loud. I could hear him from where I stood near the big front door.

"Gather up your things, boys." They had already filled the wagon with sacks of oats and harnesses and things from the shed. The rest of us had to walk while Papa and Sam rode in the wagon that Blackie pulled to our new home. Sam had to steady all the packs with his hands, arms, and legs spread out in all directions, bracing them, while Papa controlled the reins.

I felt dumb, walking, carrying our stuff. We must have looked silly to the neighbors. I hunched my shoulders and tried to make myself look small.

I guess Bella didn't care how we looked. She skipped and stomped along. Her boots made scraping sounds on the sidewalk.

Mama, from the head of our sorry procession turned and told Abraham, "Make her stop wearing out her shoes."

He walked back to Bella, took her bundle from her by its string, added it to his own in one hand. With his other hand he took Bella's. She looked up at him with a grin. He smiled back and they walked on, happy together.

I scrunched myself more and tried not to make any noise to call attention to our group.

The houses on our new block sat close together. Every one had a small front lawn of green grass, not dirt like the old house. Along the sides of each home a long driveway led to the back of the yard where the horse sheds leaned against the rear fence.

I thought our new house looked beautiful. Nice sturdy cement steps led up to the front porch, not like the wooden steps of our old home. Along each side of these steps, like a banister, was a wide strip of cement sloping down, ending in a curl up. Oh how pretty that looked.

But even prettier grew two huge hydrangea bushes on either side of the porch. They both bloomed with masses of white blossoms.

Maybe because of those flowers the whole front of the house looked rich and happy. On the sides of the lawns we saw bushes with four-o'clock flowers that opened in the afternoon, as we soon found out that afternoon when the red and pink little flowers opened up to welcome us to our new home.

Bella and I shared a bedroom like in our old house. The boys had the other, also like in our old house. Mama and Papa slept in fold-down couches in the front room here, too, but with a difference. I found out when I heard Mama complain.

"Louis, this house is …a house. Like any other house. It isn't bigger. Newer, maybe. A pull-chain toilet in a bathroom, A better kitchen, maybe. A bigger ice box. But where's the more room?"

"Come. I'll show you." Papa took Mama's hand and led her through the kitchen to the large back porch with a roof held up at the four corners by sturdy posts. "Can't you see it? All we need is to extend the walls. There are the windows already." He waved his hand around. "Sam and Abraham are old enough to help and we'll have it done before you can say Jack Robinson."

"Hm." Mama paced off the area.

"The boys will sleep here. We'll be back in the other bedroom. Soon. You'll see. Let's test the new stove now. You'll make a brisket for supper. I'll light the stove for you."

Papa was right. In a short time, and with the help of men that Papa hired, the walls went up, and the windows were set in. Our life felt good in the new house.

"I want my sisters should see how we live here, in a separate house," Mama told Papa. "Can we get the photographer again?"

He'd nodded, and that's why now Mama was pulling on my hair.

"Ouch!"

"You should look nice for your aunties and your Bubbe. Let me put this ribbon in your nice hair. Stand still."

I had to admit when I looked in the mirror I saw a prettier girl than before I'd put on my new white dress, and Mama pulled back my hair with a big puff of a white ribbon that showed on either side of my face.

Mama kept Bella's straight hair in a short bob. She didn't cry when Mama attached two puffs on either side of her hair. She once told me she thought my light, wispy hair looked prettier, but I thought hers, so thick, so dark, looked much better than mine. Mama dressed us both in matching lacy white dresses.

"This is important we should show them back home." Papa looked proud of how far we'd come. He wanted to show his own Mama back in Austria, as well as Mama's family in New York.

He bought the boys new suits. Papa wore his good dark suit. All three of them wore matching neckties.

The photographer stood ready, his head beneath the black curtain around his camera.

"Wait!" Papa yelled out that we weren't ready. The photographer uncovered his head.

We need to show them bouquets." He moved to the far hydrangea bush, the one that wouldn't show in the photograph. He picked us each a nice handful of blossoms to hold in front of us for the picture.

"I don't want one." Mama pushed away the ones he'd picked for her. "Don't you think it makes us look like we're at a funeral?"

"Really?" Papa wasn't sure now.

"I think the flowers add a touch." The photographer looked anxious to get the picture taking over with. "Stand together now."

The sun hit me right in the eye and I squinted when the photographer pushed the bulb to take the photo. I knew my part wouldn't come out good. And I was right. But Bella looked adorable and the boys looked handsome. Too bad they had to get back into their knickers for school with their old shirts and raggedy socks inside worn-down shoes.

A letter came for Mama from Tante Becky. They planned to buy tickets to come to California next summer. I couldn't read the writing because Tante Becky wrote in Yiddish

Papa found a small synagogue on Central Avenue near our new house. He didn't go often because he was so busy selling produce to make money for our family. But he wanted Sam and Abraham to learn Hebrew. My brothers went after school on days when they weren't working on the wagon with Papa or to work at the stand he also kept on a corner downtown.

I sneaked their books out of their bedroom after I finished my own homework. I tried tracing the Hebrew letters. But I didn't know what they meant. Maybe I'd ask Sam to tell me. I was afraid he'd say no. Except he liked to teach me what he learned in his history classes—about Peter Stuyvesant in New York and Father Junipero Serra here in California.. So maybe he'd help me.

Mama caught me looking at his Hebrew book which I closed fast.

"Come with me, Celia. I'll teach you Yiddish. Sounds like Hebrew. Here. Let's start with Tante Beckie's letter. Sit down in the kitchen with me."

"But, Mama, these letters aren't like the ones in my brothers' books."

"Yes, they really are. My own papa and my mama in Lithuania, they taught me. All the same like your handwriting and printing. Same letters, but look a little different. We start with aleph bes like a, b, c."

Mama learned so much English, she now could read in two languages. I told Bella that night at bedtime, "Do you want to learn Hebrew and Yiddish, like me?"

"That's okay. I have enough to work on in school."

"Don't you think it's great that Mama knows so much?" I twirled round in a circle on the floor in front of my bed."

"Sure. Gracie's mother never learned to write any language."

"Really?"

"But she's a good cook. Gracie's mom lets me eat with them sometimes. She makes great apple cake."

The letter mama received from home told her of all the things her sister sewed and knitted for them to wear in California. So many months before they could get here so they had plenty of time to prepare what to bring.

We all got excited. Mama and Papa told us the date. I marked it on my calendar with my red pencil. Mama cleaned, forced me and Bella to make our room look perfect. She and Papa went back to the couches in the living room because they would give Aunt and Uncle the bedroom. But she didn't mind this time. Cousin Isaac would sleep with the boys in the converted porch.

"Papa, can I go with you to the station to pick them up? I asked. I knew Mama had to stay home to cook. No room for all of us in the wagon. Bella and Abraham would stay home and help Mama shine up the ebony furniture even more than she'd already made all the wood shine.

"You don't want to stay and help us?" Bella asked.

"No. I want to see Tante right away."

"And Isaac," she said. "Right? Right?"

I didn't have to answer because Papa said yes.

"Celia, you can sit on the bench with Auntie. Uncle Jacob and Isaac will sit in the back with their trunks. Sam will sit up front with me."

We hitched Blackie between two automobiles at the station.

"Pa, when can we get one of these?" Sam helped me down, but kept his eyes on the sporty green and yellow Oldsmobile.

"Be patient. Remember. Next year at the latest. Get that messenger job and we can get the auto faster, Sam."

My voice went high up with wonder. "Does Mama know we're going to get one?" The very thought made me skip up and down.

The train whistle sounded. Uh oh. The blare got louder when the thunder of the train approached us. I ran back and stood behind Papa. Always a safe harbor for me.

If only he hadn't worn his good shoes to the station. His good leather shoes with thin soles, instead of his heavy work boots.

Chapter 4

At The Station, At Home, Sorrow

The monster train finally roared to a stop, but not before it filled the air around us with black smoke. When the deafening whistles, hisses, screeches quieted down, I crept out from behind Papa to join the others on the platform who were searching the mob of passengers streaming out. The wooden platform shook from all the footfalls. Each time I felt a shake I held Papa's hand to steady myself.

"There they are." Sam, the first to spot them, pointed to the crowded open door in the side of the train.

Tante Becky led the way, clunking down the steps, holding fast to the conductor's guiding hand. With two fingers of her other hand she held up her skirts. A huge cloth bag swung out from her arm. Uncle followed, loaded down with suitcases. Isaac jumped down behind, crashed into total strangers, sprinted toward us.

Papa shook hands with Uncle while Tante Becky knelt in front of me, told me what I knew she'd say, "How big you've grown." Isaac and Sam shadow boxed each other. That's the way boys greet each other every time it seems.

Papa said, "The wagon's not far. Let me help you with that." He reached down to grab one of the family's suitcases. He stepped out toward it, let out a sharp cry. His shoe landed smack onto a sharp nail sticking out of the platform.

"It's nothing." He dropped the suitcase, yanked his foot up to free it from the board.

Papa favored one foot, so everyone wanted to help him, but he waved us off. He picked up the suitcase in one hand, another bag under his other arm, limped down from the platform to the road with all the carriages. Auntie clucked her tongue.

Isaac came over to me and gave me a push to start a play fight. I laughed to show I wasn't mad when I said, "Sit down and leave me alone." I acted all ladylike on the bench. But I turned around to smile at Isaac more than once. He smiled back.

When we got home Papa unhitched our horse. "Take Blackie to the stable, Sam."

"Why do youse call him Blackie?" Isaac asked me. He didn't wait for me to explain, jumped down, landed flat on two feet with a thud.

"We just do. Come on in the back."

I heard him mutter something like that's dumb, but I turned to help Auntie down.

We gathered in the back yard

Abraham came out for his turn to get play-punched by Isaac. Abraham held his hand up to his face to fend off the greeting punches. They both laughed, so I figured this was their way of saying happy to see you. Even Bella gave a happy laugh when Isaac reached down to pat her on the back.

Next, Mama ran down the back steps, her turn to hug Isaac. I was glad to see at least he didn't punch my mom, who is his Aunt Esther. After more hugs all around Mama ushered us all inside the house.

The minute I walked in the house I was reminded that it was a Friday night. The house was prepared for the Sabbath. A clean white tablecloth covered the table. Our best silver candlesticks stood ready to be lit.

"Do you remember the prayers, Isaac?" His father asked.

Isaac shrugged.

"Help him remember, boys," Mama urged my brothers.

"I'll start." Papa began, then those who knew the Hebrew words joined in. Isaac mumbled, pretended to know the words, but he didn't. Sam and Abe looked down to hide their smiles.

I watched Mama move her hands around the flames to gather in and welcome the Sabbath. She didn't do this every Friday night but I knew Papa liked it when she did. The only light now came from the candles because outside, twilight turned to night. This hushed, musical speaking in a dark room created a solemn feeling. The candles, the prayers, the sudden quiet made our visit by the relatives special. I knew theirs would be a good visit. So I thought.

"Your soup is delicious." Aunt Becky said the same thing about all the foods Mama brought out after the soup. Bella and I giggled because we knew Mama always cooked such tasty dishes. Maybe Tante Becky never had food this good in New York.

"You'll come on the wagon with me tomorrow, Jacob. I'll show you the route."

"Louis, they just got here. Let him rest up a day."

"No, no," Uncle Jacob said. "I'll be fine. Let me see how this Los Angels is like."

Uncle Jacob didn't say Angeles. He said 'angels-ease.'. Ha ha.

Before Papa got ready for bed he soaked his injured foot in a bucket of water. Mama found some Mercurochrome to put on the part where the nail pierced the bottom of his foot. They'd already put all the kids to bed, but I was too excited to go right to sleep. I heard Papa tell Mama in a soft voice how he stepped on a nail that poked clear through the sole of the dress shoes, into his foot. "If only you'd worn your work boots," Mama said.

I slipped out from the covers, tiptoed into the room where my parents talked quietly.

"Papa, can I get you a glass of water?

"No, Dear. I have water." He pointed to a glass on the table next to him. "Come here, Celia." Papa kissed me. "Celia, you are my good girl. I'm very proud of you."

His words made me blush. I quickly said, "Bella's good, too."

Mama, from standing above me, smiled. She nodded at me.

"Of course," Papa said. "Both my *maidlach*. One more kiss now."

I went back to bed, fell asleep right away.

Papa and Uncle Jacob had already left for work before I got up the next day. I found Mama and Aunt Becky at the kitchen table talking, talking, talking. Mama barely took time out from talking with her sister to make me and Bella breakfast.

House guests weren't enough to keep Bella from running out to get Gracie to come over. Gracie came right with us to show Isaac all the things in our house, our yard and out in front. He liked the pictures on our shelves, the books in our room, the noisy wooden steps we jumped down from in the back, extra harnesses, ropes and tools in the shed, but mostly we showed off our orange trees and our neighbor's lemon and the loquat trees over the fence. In front we showed him the funny sloping areas by our porch.

Gracie looked up at Isaac. "Do you want to play a game?" Strange kids never bothered her. She didn't hang back the way I did with new people.

"What do youse play? Youse got any good games?"

Bella, like her friend Gracie, wasn't shy, either. She didn't stop to think before telling him outright, "You talk funny, Isaac."

Gracie put her hands on her hips. "Ha ha. Bella. That's just the same as you talked when you first came to my house to play."

"I did?"

"No," I butted in. "She didn't."

"You all did, especially Sam."

I put my hands over my face. How embarrassing.

Isaac walked toward the backyard. Over his shoulder he said, "How come Sam and Abe ain't here? I wanna play wit dem."

Bella ran after him. "They went with Papa and Uncle. They help sell the fruit. You ever eat an avocado?"

"Sure. Alla time."

"But Mama said we only eat them in California."

"Bella, shut up." I walked toward a box Abraham kept some old balls in. "Let's play with these."

"I'll throw." Gracie ran over. She was such a good player. Isaac wouldn't mind playing with girls if she was in the game.

Long before dinnertime we watched the horse and wagon pull up in front of the house. I threw the ball down. Papa got out real slow. He walked like he was crippled into the house. Abraham took Blackie out back to brush and feed him. Uncle and Sam brought the left-over vegetables into the house.

"Make Louis some tea," Jacob said. "He doesn't feel well."

Mama felt his forehead. "So hot, Louis. Go lay down. No, I'll get the bucket. You need to soak some more your foot."

The next day Papa stayed home on the couch with his sore foot up. Sam knew Papa's route. Uncle Jacob and Isaac went with him. Abe stayed home to help with the chores Papa usually did, cleaning the horse shed and so forth.

The next day the doctor came. The day after that the Rabbi came. And the next day two men came and took Papa to the hospital in a car.

All those days are kind of a blur to me. But I can't forget seeing Bella run after the men who carried Papa out the front door, down the steps.

"Papa! Papa!" Bella screamed as the car drove away. She leaned toward the car, reaching toward it with both hands outstretched, crying non-stop.

"Go get her," both my aunt and Mama told us kids I stood still. Sam started, but Abraham was the one who reached her first. He grabbed Bella by the waist, lifted her up.

"Wave!" He shouted, "Wave to Papa. He'll see that."

She squirmed, held out an arm, waved her hand back and forth.

Abraham set Bella on her feet. I came up to her to say in a soft voice, "I saw Papa turn and wave back to you, Bella."

"Did he?" Bella asked in between her sobs.

"I saw it, too." Abraham straightened Bella's rumpled skirt.

Sam brought the horse and cart around the front to take Mama to the hospital to stay with Papa.

In that blur of days the house seemed to fill up with people from morning to night. The neighbors, Mr. and Mrs. Raphael who were good friends with Papa and Mama, Gracie's mother and father, the rabbi, men from the produce market where Papa got his merchandise, and so many others I didn't even know.

"Go out and play, children," one grownup or another told us. We did go outside, but we didn't really play. We sat around on the porch and said stupid stuff to each other.

I went inside for a minute to get a drink of water. I heard a motor, looked out the window. A car pulled up, a man came around to Mama's side and helped her out.

She walked past the younger children, grabbed her oldest, Sam, by his arm, leaned on him up the stairs, right into the bedroom Aunt and Uncle had been using. She lay down on the bed.

I knew it. I knew what happened to Papa. They didn't have to tell me.

Aunt Becky talked to the man who drove the car, then asked the rest of us to come to Mama's room.

Mama sat up and told us the sad news that Papa died at the hospital. Even though I knew that was coming, I cried as hard as the others. Bella climbed up on the bed next to Mama, snuggled under her arm.

Sam stood against the wall. When he was helping Mama up the stairs I noticed how tall he looked. He was fourteen going on fifteen and now he looked older to me. He stood so straight you could see his pant legs ended too high above his stockings. I wondered if Mama noticed that. Sam's eyes looked red, and he kept his mouth shut tight, stared straight ahead.

Abraham ran out of the room, down the stairs and out the front door. We didn't see him again for a long time that black day.

I left Mama's side, shut myself up in my room, fell on the covers of my bed to cry alone. I needed to think. I suddenly remembered my turquoise ring. I got up and found it under my lace handkerchief. It didn't fit on my finger anymore. Papa gave me that ring made by the Indians. I kissed it and put it back in my drawer.

That night the house filled up with the more people than I'd ever seen before.

When I finally came out of my room Sam took me aside. "I saw blood on Mom's handkerchief," he whispered to me.

"What do you think she has? Isn't it just from crying?'

He shrugged.

I tried to see Mama but the table in front of the chair where she sat against the far wall blocked my view. The friends and relatives had piled the table high with all kinds of cookies, strudel, cakes, kugels, meat, chicken, breads—challah, rye bread, chopped liver, herring.—things I usually loved. This time nothing looked good to me. But the men crowding around the table, who blocked my view of Mama, had no trouble with all that food. Everyone filled plates then sat around to talk in quiet voices. Tante worked her way out of the kitchen, loaded the table with more platters.

I scooted my way around those people until I stood right in front of Mama. Abe, from behind her, put his arm around the back of her chair. Bella rested her head on Mama's lap. When Mama looked up at me she held out her hand with its wet handkerchief clenched inside. I hugged her. At the same time I craned my head toward the hand with the hankie. She held it so tight in her hand I couldn't see blood.

"Celia, Celia, my little girl, my poor children," Mama sobbed out to me. My tears flowed with the rest of our little family's. We all gave in to our grief.

Chapter 5

The Funeral ... Later, "The Home"

"Yes, Tante Becky, Mama has a black dress."

When all the guests went home and silence filled the house, I led Tante Becky by the hand to Mama's closet. We whispered because Mama was asleep on the bed across from the clothes closet, her face calm at last.

When we opened the closet door I missed the smell of Eucalyptus pods like we had at our old house. We pushed aside some dresses until we found the long dress Mama wore for good occasions.

Tante Becky yanked it off the hanger. This will do. We can cut off those bows and silver buttons so it won't look so fancy."

I let out a long breath, "Okay."

"You can wear your brown coat with a black band around the sleeve."

Oh, how awful. If only I had a black dress. But I didn't. Well, I knew I'd do what they wanted.

A voice from the bed startled us. "Buy the boys black suits, Use the money Papa put away for the automobile." Her voice was strained and creaky. "Sam knows where Papa kept the jar"

We rushed over to Mama. She looked asleep with her eyes still closed.

"Buy a little big so they can grow." She turned over on her side.

"Mama?"

She didn't answer, so we tiptoed to the door. Then she called out, "Ask Mrs. Matlin if she got black dresses that fit my girls, I need to sleep now."

Tante Becky had met Mrs. Matlin when she came to our house in the afternoon, She had nine children—mostly girls—that's why Mama figured she might have dresses from hand-me-downs. She did.

We rode to the cemetery in the funeral parlor's long black car. My family and Isaac's scrunched all together, not comfortable, Velvet curtains covered the windows, Uncle Jacob pulled one aside, Outside we saw a dark and misty sky, "Of course," Uncle Jacob said, "The weather knows, feels sad, too. It's always like this the day of a funeral."

Tante Becky poked him. "Don't be silly, Sometimes people die in summer, you know."

Uncle Jacob shook his head, looked out, up. Gray clouds, but no sign of rain.

So many friends of Papa crowded around us in the cemetery. The men, all dressed in black suits, black coats, hats with turned down brims, some old men, some young, all stood silent, their heads lowered. I couldn't tell one from another. The women, also mostly in black, fussed around, whispered, nodded. Some caught my eye to smile sadly at me, I looked away.

We four children had to stand right in front with Mama. I held Bella's hand, There before us, so close we could almost fall in, I saw the deep, empty hole, like a bathtub, with mounds of dirt all around. Across from us, on the far side of the hole, lay the plain coffin with Papa inside. Papa had to wait for the ceremony to be over before he could be laid to rest. I stood so still I thought I could hear bones creaking.

Then the prayers started. Mumble mumble. The Hebrew words became singsong sounds to me. Every so often the chorus ended and a few lone voices chanted the prayers, I should not have been surprised when I heard Abe and Sam chant in clear voices, but somehow I didn't expect that they'd know what to say. Oh, I looked behind them and saw the rabbi, coaching them.

An English prayer now—a psalm. I knew the words but I had no voice to bring them out of my chest. Besides, the sound of all the ladies' sobs drowned out most of the words.

I felt a jerk on my hand, Bella plunged forward. I screamed when her hand let loose from mine. She fell, towards the deep hole, but landed a little bit away on a patch of wet grass,

A crush of people, Mama included, all reached for Bella. She'd fainted and lay on the ground so still. Hands, hands, hands. Black sleeves, all reached for my little sister.

"Take her away," Mama said. "We need to bury Louis. A baby shouldn't see such a sight."

Uncle Jacob picked up Bella to carry her out. I saw her eyes open over his shoulder as he bounded with her toward the car. She missed the lowering of the coffin with ropes. Good thing Bella wasn't there to see big clumps of earth that people threw down on Papa in his box,

That dirt can't hurt you, Papa. And if it makes you warm, Papa, then I guess you'll feel all right.

The Home

The doctor came to check on Mama all the time now. Mama stayed in the bedroom, mostly lying down. Aunt and Uncle took over the fold-down bed in the front room. They enrolled Isaac in our school.

When I came home for lunch I saw Mama trying to cook in the kitchen. Tante Becky wrung her hands and tried to help. Tante's cooking didn't taste quite as good as Mama's but she had the strength to try when Mama felt weak

Oops. I watched a frying pan slip out of Mama's hand, crash onto the floor. Tante Becky picked it up, set it on the stove.

"Let me do it." Mama pushed Tante aside and floured pieces of fish, but she was too weak to do more.

"Can I help?" I couldn't stand to just watch.

"No, no Celia. Do your homework."

Mama nodded at me, sat down on a chair. Tante Becky placed the fish in melted chicken fat in the same pan that had dropped on the floor.

Over the next few days we did have plenty of food How good that the neighbors brought so many cooked dishes to feed us all.

Lots of other people I didn't know came to the house. One day a nice man took me and Bella aside.

"How are you doing in school?" Just one of the questions he asked.

He said his name was Doctor Frey, The way he said it, "Fry" sounded like frying fish. He had a big mustache, kind of curled up on each end. His hair looked thick and black. Clumps of it came down on his forehead. His nose looked like he had a ball on the end. The skin on his face had little holes. But I liked his eyes, Round, watery, dark.

Bella asked him, "Are you another doctor for Mama?"

"No, your mother doesn't need me. She already has a good doctor. I have young patients like you two." When he smiled he showed us nice white teeth.

"I need to talk to your mother again. He held out his hand. Oh, I guessed we should shake hands with him. Bella did first. She shook this doctor's hand up and down, high and low. The two of them laughed, and I shook his hand calmly, like a real lady and I went back to Mama's room.

When we came back from school the next day Tante Becky told

us we had to go talk to Mama in her room, Isaac wasn't allowed to go with us. I think Mama felt upset that Tante Becky bought her son a black suit with Papa's money when she got Sam and Abraham's. "That's what Papa would have wanted," I told Mama. "He was always real generous. Remember?" I wasn't sure if Mama agreed with me, but she smiled and nodded.

When Abraham, Sam, Bella and I grouped around her bed Mama spoke to us in the same solemn voice that she used with those awful words, "Papa is no more."

"The doctor told me I have to go away for a while."

"Where, Mama?"

"To a sanatorium, but a nice one. Not a hospital. A place where I'll get well."

"Mama," Bella bent close to her. "Do you have blood poisoning like Papa had in his foot?"

"No." Mama's hand came up to her mouth. I saw her spit into her handkerchief, I couldn't tell if her spitting went with her sickness and coughing, or did she spit to make bad news go away. I felt scared to ask. In the old country, she told me, they said poo poo to make the evil eye go away. But Mama didn't believe those grandmother's tales.

Abraham finally spoke. "How long will you be gone?"

"Not long. As soon as I get well I'll come back."

Bella looked more scared than me. "Will Tante Becky take care of us?" She said.

"This is what I need to tell you. No. Aunt and Uncle can't do it. They don't know how to take care of so many children. Abraham will stay here and finish school like Papa wanted.

"And me?" Sam who stood there frowning without saying a word finally asked. "What about high school?"

"You'll need to help Uncle with Papa's route while I'm gone. You can start high school again when I come home."

"But I won't be with my class."

"You're a smart boy. You'll catch up." She moved her faded blue quilt around her, making folds and wrinkles.

Sam marched out, slammed the door.

Neither Bella nor I asked the question we wanted to, what about us? We waited. Bella stood on one foot then the other. I went to Mama and stroked her hair.

That's when Mama started to cry, "They'll let me come visit you on Sundays. When I get well." She started to sob too much, she coughed again.

"Visit us? Where?"

"Do you remember that nice man, Dr. Frey? He's the superintendent for the Jewish Orphan's home. They honor us, *kinderlach*, and such an honor, that he came to our house. He doesn't usually make home visits.

I scrunched into myself. I couldn't talk. My throat tightened, hurt.

Bella had no fear. She screamed, "Orphan? We still have you, Mama. You said you're coming back. We aren't orphans just because our Papa died." Then she started bawling more than Mama.

Abraham hugged Bella, "You're my sister. I'll take care of you. Don't worry."

Bella's sobs came out slower and slower. I knew Abraham thought he should take Papa's place. Of course he never could, but how kind of him to try.

Tante Becky pulled out my top dresser drawer.

"You'll need all your underwear," she said.

I always folded my clothes in neat stacks. She picked up my folded underclothes, set them on top of my dresses already packed in the black cardboard suitcase on my bed. What would she do when she came to Bella's dresser? Bella threw her clothes in any which way. Would Tante Becky shove them in her suitcase the way she found them or would she fold them the way I did?

"I think that's all you'll be needing." Aunt Becky closed my closet.

"No!" I flung it open. "You forgot the raincoats."

"I don't think you'll need them, Not so much rain in California.. You can see that there's no more room ..."

"There's room! I'll make room. I threw myself on the clothes to smash them down inside the suitcase

"But..."

"The raincoats, Papa bought them for Bella and me for presents from him. We've got to take Papa's gifts with us!"

Tante Becky's voice came out a big long sigh. "Okay, all right. Take them."

Dr. Frey sent a car for us. Uncle Jacob put us in the back seat. Aunt Becky stayed in the house with Mama who used up one handkerchief after another to cry and cough in. A man with a funny fur hat drove. We could see him up in the front seat because the late evening light sky had not yet turned dark.

Bella and I sat still as mice in the back. We didn't move, we didn't talk, we watched the houses pass by out the windows. After a while Bella put her mouth to my ear, "His hat looks like that Russian one we saw when we peeked into Uncle Jacob's things."

"Does not," I whispered.

"Does too." She poked me.

I pushed her hand down.

She put it up, poked me again.

I twisted around, tickled her.

She laughed and pushed back at me.

I leaned into her and tickled her good.

"What goes on there in back? The driver turned his head around.

"Nothing."

We crossed our hands on our laps, stayed still again.

What I remember most about our arrival at "The Home" were stairs. We arrived when twilight had turned to dark night, The big round moon shone down on the marble steps leading to the entrance. Then, inside, the electric lighting fell on highly polished wooden stairs.

I had not climbed stairs since way back when I was little. We lived high up in a rickety old building in New York. I didn't think I'd climb up stairs again until high school. My first schools were made up of long one-story buildings; the houses I lived in were all one story. This was the first building I came to in California where I had to climb way up to get to my room.

I say my "room" – twelve beds in two rows. One had to be mine. Twelve girls slept in twelve beds, six in a row.

A lady wearing full skirts, an apron, a white hat over her bun, round eyeglasses, walked ahead of us up the stairs.

"You can call me Mrs. Mack," the lady said. "This will be your bed, Celia." She pointed to one at the far end. In most of the other beds I could dimly make out sleeping girls under thin blankets.

Then Mrs. Mack walked to one closer to the door. "Bella will sleep here."

"Oh, Mrs. Mack. She needs to sleep next to me. Can't you put her next to me? You see, we … uh, we're sisters."

"Well don't I know you are? But there's none vacant. We like to keep the little ones together, you see."

"Please." I glanced down at Bella. She had her finger in her mouth, I never saw her do that since she was a toddler. Usually not a bit shy, she now seemed to shrink into the floor.

"We really need to be together. Honest." I pleaded. Maybe it was more for my sake than for Bella's, but it was wrong to separate us. I went from scared, to sad, to really mad. "Yes, we do." Now my voice sounded angry. I surprised myself to hear me talk that way. But it was good.

Mrs. Mack looked at me,

"I guess I can wheel that one across the aisle next to you.

I didn't wait, but zoomed across the room, got hold of the empty bed by its metal frame, squeezed it in between the one on the end and the one next to it.

"Alice," Mrs. Mack said, "These are the new girls. Show them how to get ready for bed." She turned her back on us, left the room.

A very tall, much older girl, with loose, long, brown hair that flowed over the collar of her cotton nightgown, had watched us from her bed since we got there. She said, "I'll show you the bathrooms, and where to keep your clothes. Did you bring toothbrushes?"

I don't know what I would have done if not for Alice. She was so nice.

When we finally got settled under our blankets Bella found her voice. She said, "Alice, our mom's going to visit on Sundays when she gets well. We won't be here long."

"Uh huh"

"It could be soon."

"That's nice. Now see if you can go to sleep."

"Does your mom come on Sundays?"

By this time all our talking had woken up some of the girls near our beds. One started to laugh.

"What's so funny?" I tried to protect Bella.

"She don't have a mom, She been here all her life."

"That's just Ethel," Alice said, "She doesn't know how to be nice. Don't pay attention to her."

I whispered, "Is it true?"

A girl from across the room called out, "How could she have been? This is a new building. No one's been here very long."

"I mean from before the fire." Ethel sat up in her bed, her arms on her hips.

"There was a fire?" Now I was really puzzled.

Mrs. Mack burst into the room. "All of you. Back to sleep. Now."

Alice tucked me and Bella back in under our covers, She whispered to me, "I'll tell you about it later. And ..." Her whisper turned even softer, "I'll show you a photograph of my parents some day. They were beautiful."

Chapter 6

The Home. Get Used to It

I heard strange, rustling noises when I woke up in a strange bed the next morning. My eyes blinked open. The first things I saw were Bella's great big eyes staring at me from the bed where she lay on her side facing me.

"How long have you been awake?"

"A long time. I was waiting for you."

"Do you think we should get up?" By now I noticed the other girls mostly dressed, brushing hair, buttoning blouses, heading to the door.

A hand tapped my shoulder.

"At last," Alice had me sit up in bed. "You'll need to go down to breakfast, so hurry up and get dressed. I'll show you where to go."

She smoothed out my rumpled covers, added, "Tomorrow you'll have to wake up when the chimes sound and make your beds."

The stairs down didn't look so shined up and scary this morning. Light from the windows on both floors came in and took away the shadows, but I still felt dim and dark inside. Just to be there.

By the time Alice showed us where to sit in the dining room most of the girls had taken their dishes to the kitchen through a door to the side. Oof. That Ethel bumped into my chair with her hip as she headed to the kitchen, her bowl and glass held out in front of her. It had to be on purpose. Why was she this way? I never did anything to her. Most of the other girls smiled at me when I sat down.

Mrs. Mack came out of the kitchen carrying a tray with bowls of oatmeal and glasses of milk along with bread, butter, and strawberry jam. She sat down in a vacant chair in front of us.

"Dr. Frey wants to see you this morning. Alice will show you where his office is when you finish breakfast. Enjoy. And don't forget to bring us the plates when you're done. All our girls have tasks, you see."

I nodded. She got up heavily with noises, went back to the kitchen.

"Mama puts raisons in our oatmeal." Bella poked her spoon under a slice of banana on top of the cereal."

"You won't find any under there. But look. See the jam? Your favorite, Bellie."

"I bet it doesn't taste good."

I shook my head, didn't bother to try to get her to change her mind. Who cares. It might taste good. It might not. It wasn't like home.

Bella finished her food even though she said she didn't like it. I was only too glad to put our dishes in the rinsing sink in the kitchen.

Alice came for us, led us across the large front parlor, across the marble floor, away from the dining room and kitchen to the other side. She stopped by a closed door in the far wall and knocked

Dr. Frey opened the door, nodded at Alice who headed back to the kitchen. "Come, come. Girls, come in and sit down." He had us sit on two red velvet covered chairs while he sat behind his dark wooden desk. His face was just as I remembered it. A wide smile under a big mustache, bushy eyebrows, a round nose, and black hair partly hanging down on his forehead.

All along the wall behind him were shelf after shelf of books, books, and more books. Most had dark covers with a few standing out because their backs were red, green or blue between all those brown and black ones. There was a big space where one seemed to be missing.

"I see you looking at the books, Celia. Do you like to read?"

"Yes, Dr. Frey." I did remember from when he came to our house that he was nice to us, but I still felt shy. I glanced at Bella. She stared straight at him, her feet kept moving about under her chair.

"Tell me, Celia, have you ever read Dickens?"

I shook my head.

"No David Copperfield? No Oliver Twist?"

Another shake.

"Have you ever read Bronte? Of course not. No Jane Eyre I suppose."

I was a good reader, so it made me feel little to have to say no to him.

"You'll get a good education now. Our children go to public school, I want you should know. California has excellent schools."

Bella piped up, "Our school is in California, too. So we have a good education, too."

He smiled. "Well, those books I mentioned are about orphan homes. But they don't treat the children well in those stories."

"Oh, I know about orphans," Bella said. "They don't get enough food and they wear all raggedy clothes. Like Little Orphan Annie did. But we're not orphans, you know. Our mama is just sick."

"Yes, I know. And when she gets well you will go home. I just wanted to tell you we treat our children very well here. We want you should be clean and neat and learn skills."

I nodded, made my face as serious-looking as I could.

"You're enrolled in Miles Avenue School. You'll start tomorrow. Alice will show you the way." He stood up.

I stood up. Bella stayed sitting, kicking her legs back and forth. It looked like she wanted to keep talking. But I took her hand; she didn't know that when he stood up we should, too.

We spent the rest of the day looking around. The boys' cottages were off to one side of our big building. A short way behind they had workshops for them to learn woodworking. Beyond that were plots of ground for gardening. The playground was for all of us. I pushed Bella on a swing until my arms got tired. I didn't look forward to the next day, being the new girl in a new school. Not my idea of fun.

It was Alice who had to walk us the few blocks to school the next morning. She looked so young. I got up enough courage to ask her, "Don't you go to school?"

"I graduated high school last year. I'm staying on till I'm eighteen. They pay me to be a helper."

"Then what?"

"We'll see." We came to the front building. "Here's the office. Show them your papers."

Bella was assigned to a younger grade class, I, to the same grade as at my old school.

Alice adjusted the buttons on Bella's coat. "I'll walk Bella to her room. Now, Celia. You have to find room 11 on your own. It's in one of those low bungalows over that way."

She walked away holding Bella's hand. Bella tuned her head to smile at me. I made a face at her, hoped Alice wouldn't see.

Now I was all alone. No kids were out of class. No noise came from any of the closed doors. This was a big school. The weather was cool. A wind blew on me, messed up my freshly combed hair. The trees on the avenue outside whistled as the wind stirred the branches.

I was supposed to be the big girl, the protector of my little sister. I was supposed to find my way in this new big new place all by myself. Sure, I could read numbers. Even Bella could do that. I took a deep breath. I had to find the number eleven on a building. I wandered around. Lost.

Just as I finally spotted a door with an eleven written in black paint above it, a loud bell rang. Kids came roaring out. From being a silent place, it was suddenly really loud. But it didn't feel any less lonesome.

I dodged the boys and girls running out. I held my arms close to my sides, slowly made my way inside, handed the teacher my enrollment papers.

"Oh, welcome, Celia. Let me find you a seat. Let's see. Helen has a place at her table. She can help you get used to our school." She walked back to her desk, read a stack of papers, ignored me.

It was just as well. I didn't feel like answering any questions. I hoped this Helen, whoever she was, didn't treat me like that Ethel.

Happier Days

The bell rang. Helen ran in along with the others, came straight to our desk. She had a cheerful smile, wore a pretty blue dress, really short, almost to her knees. Her hair was done in two little braids over her ears tied up on top of her head with long curls hanging down the back.

"You're new I can show you around what's your name?" She talked in all one breath, her voice high and sweet.

"Celia."

"Are you from out of state? I'm from Oregon."

"No, I'm from Los Angeles." I didn't think to say first I was from New York. It was that long ago.

"Let's do our assignment. Here. The teacher's talking. Be quiet."

Me? Be quiet? She's the one doing the talking.

I found paper and pencils and books in the desk compartment. We had to do definitions and spelling. Long, difficult words.

We corrected our papers because it was a pre-test. I got everything right.

"Celia! You're really smart! You didn't miss anything."

Should I tell her? Can I trust her not to tell the teacher? Okay, it wouldn't matter. I put my mouth to her ear. "These are the same words I had at my old school. This is old stuff. That's how I knew them."

She slapped her knee. That's a good one." She laughed and I laughed with her. We both giggled so much the teacher glared at us. I knew Helen would be my friend now.

At lunch we got out our sacks, walked out the door together. The home had prepared sandwiches for all the children to carry with us.

"Is there a bathroom here?" I whispered.

"I'll show you."

When I walked out of the stall to wash my hands I saw lots of girls from our class standing in front of the mirrors. They puffed up and patted at their hair. One girl took out a tiny round container of rouge. She applied tiny amounts to her cheeks and lips. I was shocked, but acted like I thought it was normal for girls our age. It wasn't, though. Helen waited for me by the sinks.

"Look," she told me. "Your hair is the same color as mine."

I looked in the mirror. "Uh huh. Kind of a mousy brown. Not blond and not dark. Not so pretty. Oh, sorry. I mean mine. Yours is very pretty.

"Well, so is yours. It's what I call a light airy brown. Come on. I'll show you where me and my friends eat lunch."

Now it's coming. We walked together to some benches. I was sure her friends would not accept me. I prepared myself mentally to be hurt.

"This is Celia," she told them, and they all smiled at me, told me their names, let me in on their gossip. Gosh. I guess knowing Helen was my way into their club. Helen was the best desk mate I could have been given.

At afternoon recess Helen ran to join her team for kickball. That's the trouble with coming to school in the middle of a term. The teams are already chosen. Which is good as far as I'm concerned. I'm not such a good player. Nobody would want me on their team anyway.

I sat down on a bench under a tree to watch. Oops. A ball landed near my feet. I kicked it back in bounds. A girl caught it with her foot. She kicked it into the middle of the game, ran over to my bench, panting. She caught her breath and asked, "Whose team do you want to be on?"

"I'm okay. Just play. I'll sit here and watch. Maybe I'll learn your rules." That way I could pretend I just didn't know the rules, not that I wasn't very good at ball.

"Look. I saw you with Helen. Join up with her team."

The teacher came over to listen. She backed up the girl. "Go stand over there. When the other team kicks, you try to be the one to kick it back."

"But..."

She took my hand and practically lifted me off the bench. I had to try. Helen nodded at me in encouragement. Our team won, but not because I was any help. Nobody yelled at me, though.

When school was over Helen walked out with me. She walked over to the opposite street than the one I needed to walk home on. She called, "See you tomorrow," and waved.

I waved back, all happy.

As I walked back to the Home I noticed two boys walking ahead of me. They lived at the Home, too, I saw. They turned in at the gate. They'd talked a bit to each other on the way, didn't pay any attention to me behind them. They reminded me of Sam and Abe. Suddenly there was no more happy smile on my face.

What were my brothers doing back at home? What was Cousin Isaac doing? How was Mama doing in her sanatorium?

I wiped away tears.

Bella's class let out earlier than mine. Alice must have come for her to take her home. Home, I said to myself. This is my home now. I'd better get used to it.

At night after we'd eaten, got in our nighties, and hopped into bed, I finally got a chance to talk quietly with Bella.

"How did you like the school?"

"My old one was nicer."

"How was your teacher?"

"Okay."

"How were the kids? Did you make any friends?"

"No. Nobody talked to me. And I ate lunch all alone."

"Oh. I'll try to look for you at lunchtime. Maybe you can eat with us."

"Us?"

"Yes, I already made some friends."

"I didn't. And I miss Gracie. Let's go to sleep." She turned over in her bed.

"Give it time," I whispered back.

Waiting for Sunday

On Saturday after breakfast I watched the bigger children go out to work in the garden. They hurried out the front door and down those steps. I noticed that behind the large front entry room there was a hall which led to several smaller rooms in the back. The littler kids jumped about, grinning, babbling to each other, seemed to know what they were doing. They ran to a playroom in the back.

I started out the door with the older girls. I guessed that was what I should do. Nobody told me anything. The older boys stood around out in front, seemed waiting to join in with the gardening. Without warning, Mrs. Mack took hold of my arm. I stopped. Did I do something wrong?

"Celia, would you like to read to the smaller children for story time?"

Oh, how could she know? There was nothing I'd rather do. "Yes, Mrs. Mack."

"Come. I'll show you where."

Maybe that's where they'd led Bella this morning. I hoped she'd be one of the kids I was going to read to. But as we passed by, out of the corner of my eye I saw that Bella was in one of the playrooms, pouring play tea from a toy dishes set to a girl seated at a small table in the corner.

Mrs. Mack took me past that door to a children's library—a room with low shelves, stuffed animals, and colorful books. The little ones gathered on a mat in front of the reading chair where I was to sit. Mrs. Mack placed a book in my hands.

I read in my clearest voice. I held the pictures up for everyone to look at. When the frog in the story talked I made my voice squeaky and funny. Good job I told myself.

Taking a moment to look away from my book I glanced at the children. Only two had their attention on me and the book. One little boy was sucking his thumb and looking at the floor. Another two boys played tug of war with a toy dog, not paying any attention to me at all.

What should I do? Should I stop reading? Should I tell them

to look up? I took a deep breath and just went ahead and read. The next time I looked up I saw Bella standing in the doorway. She made a face at me, tongue out, eyes crossed, then ran away. How could she do that? I have to keep reading. I opened the book wider. I held the pages open and ran them close to the heads of the little kids, two at a time. This worked. They looked back up and I finished the book. Phew.

"You did good. I'll play with them now." Alice came in and set me free.

Outside in the garden, I watched helplessly while those who knew what to do hoed, dug, planted, trimmed, or did whatever needed doing. I tried to figure out a task I could do. But when I lifted up a trowel and a kid pulled it out of my hand, I chose to just stand and watch.

The rest of the day dragged on. When I saw Bella across from me at dinner I got mad at her. "Why did you interrupt my reading?"

"I just wanted to make you laugh. To cheer you up."

"It wasn't funny."

"You like when I make hor'ble faces. It makes you laugh."

"That was back at home. Don't do it here."

"Sorry."

"Oh, eat your carrots."

When the next day, Sunday, came, we saw it was family day. The mothers or fathers who could visit stayed with their children out on the grounds in front.

Our Home sat at the top of a low hill. Green lawns covered all the area in front except for the circular drive and the brick path to the front door of the main building. The boys' two cottages sat to the side.

Trees with lacy branches dotted the property in artistic arrangements. Under the trees, on benches and spread-out blankets, sat small family groups.

I told Bella, "See those benches? When Mama gets better that's where we'll go sit with her on a Sunday visiting day.

"Maybe next week?"

"It's too soon. Let's go inside. We can read or do homework up in the dorm."

During the next week Bella and I each received a small package in the mail. When I got home from school my package was waiting on my bed. Bella had already opened hers.

"Oh good." Under the brown paper I'd torn open was a dainty box with purple- edged stationery with matching envelopes.

"Let's see yours. Mine is pink." Bella held up a note. "This is from Aunt Becky. It's so we can write to Mama. See? Here's the note from Auntie."

I recognized the handwriting. "Hey. That's how Abe writes. He wrote it for her. I can tell. It had to be his idea, anyway."

"Do you think so? That's okay. I'm going to write to Mama right away."

Chapter 7

Summer, a Visit, Aunt and Uncle, Ouch, Woodshop

Our mother wrote short letters to answer ours. Each time Bella or I got one we tripped over ourselves to get hold of them, tear them open.

"I think Mama will be coming out soon." Bella sat on her bed, holding her letter upside down on her lap.

"Did she say that?" I snatched her letter away, scanned it. "That's not what she said. She's only feeling better."

Bella slid down from the bed on to the floor between her bed and mine. I scrunched down next to her even though the space was so little.

I smoothed down Bella's hair on the sides. "Still, it won't be too long, I think."

The bed on my side shook. I looked up to see Ethel bumping into it.

"What do you want?" I pulled myself up and stood facing her.

"You never get visitors."

"This is a private conversation between my sister and me. You aren't needed here."

"But I only came to tell you I got your job."

"You mean in the garden?

"No, reading to the little kids. Mrs. Mack asked me."

I squinted at her. "That's cause I told her I needed to be outside more. She wanted me first."

"I don't believe you." Ethel smirked.

"That's what happened." I put my nose up in the air. "And quit following me around at school."

"I don't." Ethel walked away.

"Celia, does she really do that?" Bella took my hands in hers. She pulled at my wrists, tried to get herself up, wanted to stand beside me.

"I saw her a few times. I think she was spying on me and Helen." My eyes followed Ethel's back.

I would try to stay away from her. The only thing I could do.

"Did you really tell Mrs. Mack you didn't want to read to the little kids any more?"

"I meant to tell her." That wasn't a lie. I just hadn't got round to it yet. Those little kids didn't follow the stories like I thought they would.

"Let me help you up," I said.

Weekdays we had homework and chores. But Sundays were Visiting Day and free time for those of us with no visitors. Sunday became the hardest time for me and Bella. I often looked out the windows and saw families clustered on the lawn below.

Our letters from Mama arrived less often. One day Dr. Frey asked me to come into his office.

"Can I go with you?" Bella asked me.

"No. They said only me."

She tugged at my arm. Reaching up, she put her mouth to my ear. "Do you think Mama's dead, like Papa?"

"Of course not! Don't be dumb!" I scolded her. But my knees shook and my heart beat fast. I opened his office door and stepped in.

Dr. Frey, big and important looking, smiled down at me, urged me to sit.

I was so relieved to hear what he said that I could concentrate only on calming my heartbeat. This wasn't about Mama. I leaned back in the chair.

"Well, then, next Sunday your aunt and uncle will visit in the afternoon. You and your sister should put on your good dresses and meet them outside."

I was scared to ask him anything more, even though he was so nice. I didn't want to, but I knew Bella would be angry if I didn't force myself to ask. Probably I was afraid I'd hear a bad answer. But I did speak in a low voice, "What about our Mom? Can she come… with them?"

"She's not well enough, but probably in the summer she will be able to."

I nodded. That meant she was not dead like Papa, the way Bella put it. I managed to thank him and left, almost on tiptoe, out the door.

Bella stood outside, waiting for me. I laughed and told her not to worry.

At bedtime she said to me, "I wish it wasn't Tante and Uncle."

"They're okay."

"Maybe they're coming to take us home."

"I wish they would."

"I didn't think we'd have to stay here in summer vacation."

"I know what you mean, Bellie." I sighed a long breath.

"Maybe we'll have to stay here till we grow up, like Alice."

"Just shut up and go to sleep. You know that won't happen." I closed my eyes.

On Sunday we dressed with extra care. I combed Bella's thick hair and put a ribbon in it. She'd better get it cut if she wanted to keep her bob. Her hair had grown pretty long since she got here. As for my own hair, I tried making those little braids like Helen had. My hair fell about in such wisps, it wouldn't stay braided. I pushed it back behind my ears.

My first sight of Tante Becky on the bench out on the grounds was of her black high top shoes. Her skirt only came over her knees. All the ladies I could see standing about here wore their skirts shorter than mama ever did. I wondered if Mama had any new clothes in the sanitarium, if the clothes she brought kept her warm.

Uncle Isaac wore his same black suit. He held out his arms. Bella ran into them and hugged him. I hugged Tante Becky and was surprised to feel the warmth when she hugged me back. This was mama's sister, just like Bella was mine, and even though she wasn't always so good to me, I could tell she wanted to be here. I'd been afraid that Dr. Frey had forced her to visit. Still, her hug was not the same as hugging Mama.

Leave it to Bella to say straight to Tante, "How come you never visited us sooner?"

"Bella!" I was so embarrassed. "That's not a question you should ask."

Uncle answered for her, "Ask. Ask. We shouldn't leave the boys alone, you know. We have Sam and Abraham and Isaac, all needing us by them. Boys alone, who knows what kind trouble? Today they promised to be good by themselves."

"Besides," Auntie said, "They do their route on Sundays, too. People buy. They need. We sell."

Uncle started to say something, "Your papa, may he rest in peace, he left bills…" Auntie elbowed him.

"They don't need to hear such things. They are babies."

"We are not babies." Bella put her fists on her hips.

I quickly asked, "How is Mama? Do you see her?"

"Yes, at the sanitarium we visited last week. We decided we should come here to visit you."

Oh, now I understood. Must have been Mama's idea then.

Bella asked, "Could you take us to visit her?"

I pushed at her shoulder. "Of course not."

"No, dear. They don't let children."

"Is she getting well?" I asked.

"She's not coughing blood. Not so weak. She sits outside in the open air and embroiders dresser scarves for you."

"What about Sam? Can he visit her? He's older than us."

"No, no. Too young still. He writes her letters. She showed me. Stacks."

"And Abraham? Does he write too? Stacks, too?"

"Maybe. Not so high." She gestured with her hands a lower height. "He writes. I give to the mailman for him."

"Can Sam go back to school? After summer?"

She shrugged

"What about Isaac. Is he going to summer school?"

"We'll see."

Uncle reached in his pocket. "I brought candy." He pulled out little sacks of hard candies and chocolate drops. "Take."

Bella took her bag, faced him. "Can you bring Mama if you come again?"

Uncle gave her a helpless look.

Aunt Becky stood up "If your mama should only be well."

Uncle took her arm. "We are happy we could come today, little girls. But you are not so little. The short time you are here you are big already."

Bella giggled. "No we're not."

"Say thank you for the candy." I held her by both shoulders.

She squirmed free of my arms. "Why don't you say thank you yourself, Celia?"

"I did." At least I'd meant to.

"You're welcome. So welcome." He made it sound like "velcome."

Then the visit was over.

Later, up in the dorm, Bella ran over to her friend Louise, whose bed sat at the other end of the room. "We had visitors today," I heard her say in a proud voice. The two girls whispered together, then the noise of them giggling sounded sweet to my ears.

I was glad Bella had finally made a friend here. I wished that my friend Helen was here. No! I didn't mean that wish. Let her stay with her family. Not here!

Dr. Frey stood up at the head of the breakfast tables to make an announcement. He told us that we would all be enrolling in summer school. Some would be taking over subjects they failed. That wasn't Bella and me. We both got good grades. We'd be with the ones who took art and music. Great. Now I'd have something good to write to Mama about.

At school Helen ran up to me, all smiley and happy. She pushed me in through the doorway on the way to our seats.

"Guess what."

"What? Tell me?"

"I get to go to summer school. Please please you, too, so we can be together."

"I do get to go." My voice didn't sound happy like hers.

"Don't you want to?"

I wished I could tell her about wanting to be home by summer. Instead I said,

"Well, it's only in the mornings."

"I know. But maybe you can come over to my house and play in the afternoon."

I stammered, "Maybe."

But I would not go to her house. I didn't know if they'd let me, but even if they did I wouldn't go. Because then she'd want to come to my house. I sure didn't want her to know I lived in an orphan's home.

I busied myself with my books.

Needlework, Garden, Woodshop

I got to see Helen quite a bit in summer. We shared long recesses where we played ball with her friends, who were now my friends, too. We sat next to each other in Art class.

"Quit making fun of my drawing," I whispered to her.

"It's just that if it's supposed to be a tree, it looks like a telephone pole," she told me when I sketched out an oak.

"Wait till I fill in the leaves. Where's some green?"

She reached into her paint tray, pulled out a round glob of green paint."

Her fingers smoothed down the edge of my clean white paper. It curled up on the edges.

I pushed her paper closer to me. I peered at it. "Well, if that's supposed to be a woman it looks like a man."

We both laughed because it was fun to sit next to together and make fun of each other's clumsy artwork.

A few times we got to eat our lunches on the playground and stay and walk around the climbing equipment and talk in the afternoon. But she never mentioned coming to her house any more. I quit holding my breath, waiting for that.

Usually I had to go right back to the Home after summer school, and take Bella with me.

I didn't know that our summers would be so busy. Good because busy made the time pass fast. More chores. I had to fold towels in the laundry room. Hot in there. But summertime made it hot outside, too.

Then there was my plot in the garden to take up time. Also, going to temple in our top floor synagogue on Friday nights, religious classes Saturday morning. Embroidery lessons for the girls and Sloyd woodworking for the boys in the afternoons after classes.

Mama wrote letters saying she was getting better all the time. Soon she would be able to pay us a visit. I stored them in their envelopes in my books. But I never re-read them. I thought of them as empty dreams.

Bella held my hand on the way home from school. We got out at the same time in summer school.

"It's too hot, Celia" She fanned herself with her limp hand. "Look at Abe. He's dragging his jacket sleeve on the ground."

In front of us a group of three boys walked along in their shirt-sleeves, laughing, bumping into each other, making noises.

"Which one's Abe?" I asked her.

"You know. That tall one."

"How come you know them?"

"Don't you know them, too? They're always in the garden with you. That Abe borrowed your rake once. Then there's Ben and Ruben and they're friends with Al and Edgar and ..."

"Stop. Now I remember. But ... you know all their names. I never even talk to them."

Bella skipped a few steps. "I know the little ones' names, too. You just never pay attention."

"Well, the teacher back home said I'm nearsighted. Remember? Besides, the boys eat in their cottages. We have our own dining room." Practically the only time we were all together was in the garden. And also in the synagogue, but even then we sat on different sides.

"Sure. But back at school we play with 'em on the playground. And some of the boys from the Home are in my class at school."

"None's in mine." I slowed my walking. They were slowing in front of us. I didn't want to bump into them.

"Hey Abe," Bella called out.

"Shh." I pulled back on her arm.

He turned around. "What you want?"

"Nothin'. I got a brother named Abe, too."

"Yeah, I know. You told me before."

"Celia's our sister."

He looked straight at me. I did remember him the time he used my rake.

"Yeah, I know." He turned back around. The others had spun around and looked at me and Bella but now they turned back. They sauntered along even slower.

We were close to the grounds of the Home. We crowded around the entrance, scrambling and hopping along like bunnies to a cabbage garden, till we got through the wrought iron gates. Then, fast, we ran to our buildings.

"Celia," Bella said when we reached the front door. "You read all the time. That's why you don't pay attention to the kids here. I go out and play while you stay inside with your books."

"I thought Louise was your only friend here."

"You never pay attention to anything. I have lots of friends here now."

When she said that I thought about how long we've been here. I always thought we'd go home soon. So it wouldn't matter if we made friends here or not.

Activities, Chores

"Ouch!" Bella held up her finger. "I stabbed myself."

She put her finger in her mouth, took it out and examined it, then held it out again for all the girls to see. The girls around her in our embroidery circle looked up from their stitching, stared at her. Mrs. Mack got up from her seat in the middle, waddled over to Bella.

First she picked up Bella's embroidery hoops surrounding the white cloth with simple black cross stitches. She peered at it to see if there was any blood on it. Only then did she take Bella's finger in her hand to see if it was bleeding. A small drop covered the pad of her finger.

"Celia. Take your sister to the infirmary to get this bandaged."

I set my own work with its neat violet and blue designs under my chair. When I got up, I had to quick step to the side to avoid bumping into another girl who brought her hoops to Mrs. Mack to ask for help on a new stitch she was teaching us.

Bella and I hurried down a corridor, around a corner and down a hall to a small room behind the kitchen. The room looked like an infirmary, with a cot, shelves holding all sorts of medicines and bandages, and a metal desk. But we found no nurse there. The only time a doctor or nurse came was when we all had to stand in line to get our shots or examinations, and then a different doctor came, and sometimes there was a nurse. But our own Doctor Frey saw to all our little bruises and cuts.

This time the cook came out of the kitchen. She looked at Bella's finger. "So you pricked your finger with a needle. Let me put alcohol on it."

"I want Doctor Frey to look at it." Bella said, her voice whiney, her mouth pouty.

"Don't be silly. He's too busy for this little thing." She poured on some red solution.

"Ouch! That burns," Bella said. "Celia, help me."

"It only lasts a minute." But I noticed that the blood still oozed out. Except that now the blood, diluted with the other liquid, appeared light pink.

The cook wiped it with cotton, wrapped gauze on it and taped it up.

"That didn't take long," she said. "Go back."

"I can't work on my project any more, can I Celia?"

'You can use your other fingers to hold the hoop, can't you?"

"Don't want to."

"Did you stab yourself on purpose?"

"No! Course not. I'm making that for Mama. I want her to have it all nice."

"Well, I'll help you with it. For Mama. Come on."

We left the infirmary. I started for the same corridor we came through before.

Bella ran away from me to the entry across the marble floor, and out the front door. "Come on, Celia. We have to see the Sloyd class. I told David, that boy in my class at school, I'd watch him. Come on. This is the best time we can."

"No. But. . . .they won't...oh, well." I followed her, gave up trying to bring her back, watched her little legs like sticks under her full skirt run on ahead.

The path around the main building to the side yard passed the two cottages and led behind them. The first cottage was the dorm the older boys stayed in. The smaller boys lived in the second cottage where their matron had her bedroom.

We trotted through their playground between the tall wooden poles where old automobile tires hung from ropes for them to swing on. Farther to the side was the dusty marked-off diamond where they could play baseball. The empty field looked sad with no one playing there, nothing moving through the still, hot air.

Beyond the swings, close to the main cottage, the garden plants shot up green leaves. I let Bella run ahead, left her alone. I tiptoed between rows to find the lettuce heads I'd planted. Great. The green heads were still plump with light green rounded leaves. The Tomato vines I'd carefully weeded last Saturday still had little fruits. Hello friends. My plants were doing good.

The other kids' plots stretched out beyond mine. A few were dry and brown. More looked leafy and thriving, like mine. Which plot was that boy Abraham's? Probably one near mine. I bent to pick a caterpillar off a leaf. I blew a kiss to my squash blossoms, bypassed the row of flowers edging the garden plots, and ran to catch up with my bold little sister.

To go along the dusty path I had to step over scattered wood chips and splinters. The path ended at a large yard. Plop in the middle of the lot stood a three-sided wooden building—a shop with an open side. Inside the shop I could see tables and tools and metal tall things and motor things. But the boys all worked on the far side of the yard. Logs and stacks of wood and rolls of wire leaned against a low fence. Most of the boys, their elbows bent, arms struggling back and forth, sawed boards balanced on saw horses. The teacher, way at the back of the yard, put one arm around the shoulders of tall boy in overalls. He held the boy's project up with his other arm. I wondered what he was telling him.

Bella called out to me from the edge of the large lot where the boys had their woodworking shop. One boy about her size, his overall strap slipped down off one shoulder, held out something small with sharp angles for her to look at.

I walked over to her, stepping carefully over wood chips and rocks and twigs and leaves.

"This is David. He's in my class."

"Okay. Hi." I waved. Some sawdust clung to the skirt of my dress. I brushed it off.

I couldn't imagine how Bella found David among all those boys of all sizes and ages.

I noticed two others, about the same size as David, both with messy hair, staring at us from the yard. One had on a short sleeved checked shirt and the other, a long sleeved flannel shirt beneath his overalls. Their thin leather shoes were covered in wood dust. Both had wrinkled, falling down socks that you could see below the bottoms of their pant legs.

Bella spotted them and motioned for them to come over. The way they shifted about and peered at us, you could tell that they were curious to come see what we were doing.

David held up his wood object. "Bella, this is a bookend. I'm making it for my Mom. When she visits." One of the other boys said, "I made one, too. Wait till you see it after I sand it some more. Then I'll varnish it. Make it shine."

"Where's yours?" David asked the third boy.

"Over on the table, drying. I finished it. Now I have to make the matching one. They're supposed to be a pair."

"Your moms will love them," I said.

The third boy turned and walked off toward the shed. I saw him put his fist to his eyes. Was he crying?

"He's Julius. He doesn't have a mom," Bella told me.

"But he's got a Dad," David said. He visits sometimes. I saw him."

"Our dad is dead," Bella said.

She didn't cry. I was surprised at how she said it so plain. When she ever mentioned our Papa to me she always had tears in her eyes. Not this time.

"Let me see your bookend," I said to David. He handed it to me. "Yes, it does need another. You do have to have a pair or the books will fall down."

"Zoom." He made motions with his hands to imitate a row of falling books.

Bella laughed, made me smile.

I took her hand. "Thanks for showing us, David. We better get back." The teacher from far across the yard looked at us, but he didn't move toward us.

Bella pulled her hand from mine, thrust her bandaged finger out for David to see.

"What happened?" He scrunched his eyes.

"I'll tell you at school tomorrow." She let me pull her along. The wood scraps crunched under our shoes.

Chapter 8

Mama at Last, Autumn, Basket

Between the end of Summer School and the new semester we had time off. Just as the time began to seem endless we got word that Mama was coming to visit at last.

Sunday morning's happy chatter at the breakfast table filled the room. Most of the kids were expected to have visitors and now Bella and I could expect one, too. So exciting that Mama would meet us on the bench. Bella and I must have pushed each other out of the way of the mirror upstairs a dozen times. Alice came in from her room to help us tie our sashes and hair ribbons. All the girls pushed for places at the mirror to check how they looked.

"Do the boys have special Sunday clothes, too?" Bella asked her.

"Most do. At least clean shirts. They have to clean their shoes, of course, and make sure their hair is combed. They look so nice when they come out the doors of the cottages." Alice turned Bella around to tighten her sash.

At last the time came for visiting hours. Everyone rushed down the stairs, out the door. I was sure Bella would jump up in Mama's lap when we found her. I planned to wait, give her a chance first, and then run to hug Mama myself.

But it was way different when we found her sitting all alone. I stopped, then looked away. I'd seen her in one glimpse and couldn't get over how she looked. Her hair was still in a bun, but the bun was lower and looser, grayer. Her skirt looked shorter and plainer. She had on beige cloth stockings and nice-looking, black, low-top shoes. But mainly Mama looked skinny now. She was not the plump Mama who always enveloped us in her arms.

I guess Bella had that same impression. She stood a few steps away from Mama with her thumb in her mouth.

Mama held out her arms, a sad smile on her face.

"Come, my babies." She started to stand up to come to us.

"No, Mama. Stay there." I stepped up and put my arms around her. She put her arms around me and we hugged and hugged. I cried, and Mama cried, too.

Bella now ran to join us. "Mama."

I moved aside to make room for Bella to hug us both. The three of us clung to each other and hugged for a long time. Finally Mama made room on the bench for Bella to sit on her right and me on her left. She bent to kiss us, first one then the other then back to kiss Bella's head on her hair. She pushed my hair back away from my face where it had gotten loose and kissed my check.

Suddenly she frowned. "Are the people nice to you here?" "How is your school here?" And a million other questions which we didn't know how to answer.

One thing I wanted to know was, "Did Sam get to go back to school."

"Oh, my darling. No. He is still delivering telegrams for Western Union. He looks so handsome in his uniform. Uncle got him a new bicycle to help him get around. He has the nicest bag. It's leather and he wears it around his neck."

"What about Abraham?"

"Still helping with the produce route. Such a good boy. He helps around the house, cuts the lawn, cleans the horse shed."

"Doesn't uncle help?"

She laughed. "Tante Becky does."

Bella stood up. "Aren't you still in the sanitarium?"

"Oh, they gave me a furlough. That means I have to go back to be tested. Every week. If my cough clears I can quit going." She got out a handkerchief then and coughed a deep loud horrible sound. "I have to wait for the all clear." She didn't show us the contents of her hankie, but stuffed it back in her plaid bag with the wooden handles.

"But we can go home and be with you, Mom." Bella said. Since when did Mama become 'Mom' I wondered. "We will take care of you."

"As soon as the doctors let me. Soon."

Bella turned aside. She looked across at other family groups. They seemed so happy. Maybe they just seemed that way.

I didn't ask about Isaac. Mama guessed that I was wondering. She said, "Isaac still doesn't like his school. He misses his old one, and the other cousins."

"If they go back to New York does that mean Bella and me can come back home?"

"The doctors. The say I can't have you yet."

We sat in silence. Bella swung her legs back and forth under the bench.

It didn't make sense to me that Mama could come and kiss us, but the doctors wouldn't let us go home with her. No sense at all.

The Sunday before school started Mama got to come visit us again. This time she brought a basket. We first sat on the same bench as on her first visit. Mama spread a blanket on the ground in front of us. She opened her basket and took out little packages. A picnic. Bella sat on a corner of the blanket, patted the place next to her. I smoothed down the skirt of my good dress and sat beside her. Mama passed out cloth napkins the same way the teacher passed out assignment papers. It made me think of how nice my teacher always was to me. Not that she was nicer than Mama. Oh, no. But I was around her more than with Mama, for almost a year already.

Our good plates. I recognized them from our china cabinet when Mama unwrapped them from newspapers. We each got one and a silver fork and then Mama unwrapped the food she brought. A chicken leg, a *pulka*, seasoned with her special salt and pepper and fried in matzo meal. A smooth dough knish with mashed potatoes inside. More good stuff and then she unwrapped slices of apple strudel. Yum.

I licked the crumbs from my fingers.

She brought out more slices wrapped in brown paper. "These are to take up to your room. You should eat all week."

"No, Mama." Bella handed the parcels back. "We're not allowed to take food to our dorm."

"Such a rule. I understand. Maybe bugs. Look. Here comes a girl. Is that your friend, Celia?"

I glanced over my shoulder. I saw, striding toward us with a sour look, Ethel. Oh no. What did she want?

Ethel planted her feet in front of our little group. She looked down at us, focused her eyes on Mama.

"Dr. Frey says to come to his office, Mrs. Heuer."

"What for? The girls, too?"

"No. He said you'll come right back."

Mama leaned her elbows on the bench seat to help boost herself up. "Pack up when you finish, girls. Be careful with the dishes. But eat first."

"I don't want any more." Bella opened the basket.

"Maybe your friend wants. You like strudel?" Mama held out a slice to Ethel.

She shook her head no. I asked her, "What does Dr. Frey want, Ethel?"

She shrugged, turned toward the building. Mama followed her.

I picked up a plate with faded-looking pink roses in a design around the edges.

"Bella, remember these? We had them in New York. I helped Mama pack them."

"I remember. We only used them for good. What do you think Dr. Frey wants to tell Mama?" She wiped a plate off with a napkin and wrapped it carefully in the now greasy paper.

"Maybe he'll say that if she's well enough to be with us here, she can be well enough at home, too. That's what I think."

"Then can we go back home?" She wrapped another plate.

"That's what I'm hoping."

The basket filled up fast with the remains of our picnic. We shook out the blanket. I tried to fold it so it would look neat, but Bella let go of her end, said, "Whee," and let it fly like a sail. "Stop that!" I grabbed it away, finished folding it, set it on top of the basket on the bench next to mama's bag with the wooden handles.

Finally we saw Mama come out the building down the path toward us. Ethel, acting all important, walked alongside her.

"I wish that girl would go back, Bella. I wish Mama would come here by herself."

"Me too."

"I try to be nice to her."

"Why?"

"Because she's a full orphan. We're only half orphans."

"Maybe that's why Dr. Frey has her be his messenger."

I frowned. "She's also his spy."

"What does he need a spy for? Do you ever do anything wrong, Celia?"

"No. Here they come. Sh."

Mama barely looked at us. She said in a high voice, "All packed?" She reached to pick up the basket. Her hands fluttered about the handle a bit before she got a grip on it.

The streetcar she needed to take stopped down at the foot of Pacific Blvd. a few feet past our gate. Wasn't she going to wait for us to walk her down there?

"Mama?" There was a question on my lips and on my raised eyebrows.

She looked at Ethel, started to say something then tugged at her bag.

I stamped my foot. "Ethel. Go back. Dr. Frey needs you."

"Celia!" Mama thought I was being rude. She didn't know Ethel was never nice to me. But my saying that to Ethel did the trick. She turned and went back.

"I try to be nice to her, Mama."

We heard a deep sigh. Mama set down the basket and sat herself back down on the bench.

"Come here next to me again, Bellie, Celia. "What did Dr Frey want you are wondering."

I nodded. Bella shook her head up and down real hard. She asked, "Did he say we can go home now?"

"No, not yet. It's about the food. He got mad I should bring you girls my home cooking. Hired nutritionists he's got. You should pardon me. I make tasty, healthy food for my girls. No. It's not scientific. They make menus here very scientific. I don't follow their guidelines. No food next time. Only the nutritionist, the latest, can make the food."

"It's not that good, Mama. Honest." I said.

"Is it enough? Do you get enough to eat?"

"Celia leaves her vegetables on her plate sometimes." Bella giggled. "But I eat mine. It's healthy they told me."

"Yeah, you eat them cause you like them."

"Do not."

"*Maidlach,* girls. The boys are waiting. I have to go. Isaac and Sam, I need to be there to see they don't fight."

"Fight? You never told me that did that. They got along good before."

"You shouldn't worry. They play. They argue. Sam argues. Abraham makes peace. Little Abraham is the peacemaker. You'll see."

"Okay, Mama."

Autumn

The next letters we got from her said she'd gone back to the sanitarium and couldn't visit for a while. But school had started. That kept me busy. Again I got to be in Helen's class.

In September a sad thing happened to Bella. I went upstairs and found her sitting on her bed with her thumb in her mouth. She hadn't done that in ages.

"It's about Louise. She was my very best friend here."

"I know." I looked over at the end bed. It was made up, sheets tight, not a wrinkle.

"She went to go live with her grandma in Oakland."

"Oh, Honey. Be happy for her. Didn't you tell me you have lots of friends here? I see you talking to everybody."

She nodded. "I told Louise to write to me."

I kissed Bella on the top of her head. "She will."

In October I got invited to Helen's Halloween party. She passed me the envelope under my desk. She watched me tear it open and read it. It said you had to wear a costume, and the party started at six o'clock. At the bottom it said to RSVP.

I didn't know what to tell her. Would they let me go? Could I get a costume? Wouldn't it be dark when the party ended?

She squeezed my hand, slipped the invitation back inside my envelope for me. "Write me your answer. Oh, Celia. I know you'll come. Write me a regular RSVP. See my address on the envelope? Address it to me. My mom wants to see who's coming. But I like to get mail in my own name."

"I like getting mail, too." But she didn't know mine came from my very own mother.

I worried about going to Halloween all through the afternoon. When I got back to the Home I told my sister all about it. "And if I write her an answer, I'd have to put my return address on the envelope. She'll know where I live."

"She won't care. She likes you."

"She'll think I'm different. It's embarrassing."

"She probably knows already. Don't you ever talk about it?"

"No. I do tell her about my brothers.. She has brothers, too. But we mostly talk about books and games and the teachers and stuff"

"Just write the street number. You don't have to write Jewish Orphan's Home on top of it.

"What if I put our old address in Los Angeles?"

"That's silly. Do you need a stamp? I have lots in my writing kit. But you better find out if they'll let you go first. Go ask Mrs. Mack."

"I guess I better."

Bella mumbled, "I wish somebody would invite me to a party."

"They will when you're older." I didn't know about that. But she'd like hearing it.

I wasn't sure if I should ask Dr. Frey or Mrs. Mack. I was suddenly afraid. It would be easier to ask Alice. I went to find her. She worked in the office now, practicing her secretarial skills. She'd have to get a job after she turned eighteen. Dr. Frey let her work filing his papers and typing on his new typewriter.

I showed her the invitation.

"I'm sure it will be all right. When Dr. Frey comes back I'll check with him."

"And the costume..."

"Do you have any long skirts and necklaces? Tie a scarf around your head and be a gypsy."

"Maybe."

I went up to my room. Each girl had a drawer in a high chest in the alcove next to our dorm. Beside that was a cupboard with a small bar to hang our clothes on. I found my long red skirt smashed in toward the back. But way in the back hung the darling raincoat Papa had bought me. Such a long time ago. I brought it out and tried it on. Good thing Mama had him buy it large. It still fit but it was short on me now. But if I wore it with the red skirt that would look like part of it. And if I put the hood up, it would be perfect. I could be Little Red Riding Hood. So much better than an ordinary gypsy. Now I got excited. Let's see ... I'd need a basket.

Most of the other children were playing outside, swinging on their playground equipment, or in the garden. Some stayed in the library.

I tiptoed into the kitchen. Empty. Cook must be in the pantry. I checked out all the shelves and counters. I saw vases and flowerpots, but no baskets. I turned around craned my neck to look on the opposite wall at the top of the highest shelf. The perfect thing. A wicker basket with woven sides and a tall twisted handle.

Under the sink I noticed the stool where Cook sat to wash the vegetables. I pulled it out and set it beneath that high shelf. It was easy to reach for the basket when I climbed up.

"You can't have that."

"What? Who said that?"

"It's me. Ethel."

"Oh, Ethel. I know I didn't ask first, but...."

"Put it back."

"I think Cook will let me use it if I ask."

"No. It belongs in the kitchen. Get down."

"What's it for?"

"I don't know, but it's for the kitchen."

"That's stupid. If it doesn't have any use…"

"Are you calling me stupid?"

"That's not what I said."

"I'm going to get you in big trouble."

"Why? What did I ever do to you?"

"Hey! Get down from there." Cook, holding bundles against her white apron, rushed in. She set down her packages of flour and sugar as she came toward me. Ethel bumped into my stool, and between the two of them the stool tipped and I fell off, the basket still in my hand.

"Ow." I landed on my side. It hurt. They reached out to help me up. I pushed Ethel's hands away and took hold of Cook's hand. I scrambled up, pretended it did not hurt.

"What are you doing?"

"I … I needed this. This basket."

"What for?"

Before I could answer we saw a shadow in the doorway. Mrs. Mack came in carrying bowls of eggs they'd gathered from the chicken coop in back.

"What's going on?"

I swallowed. I had planned to ask her permission to go to the party, but not here, not in front of these people. But now I had to.

I squeaked out, "I needed to borrow the basket. Mrs. Mack, I was invited to a party and I'm hoping it would be all right if I …"

"You mean from that girl Helen, from your school?"

"Y … yes."

"You can walk over with Abraham and Leonard. They know the way. You have to all come home together. The mother will walk you all home."

"Oh." I must have had a stupid look on my face. I didn't know Helen asked them. To hide my ignorance and my astonishment, I could only think to say, "They're in a higher grade."

"They were together in after-school groups. This Helen, she has friends in other classes, too. Her brothers have friends here. I knew their whole family."

She ran her hand down the side of my basket, testing how strong it was. "I'm going to help with the costumes. I'm giving Abraham a torn sheet. He can be a ghost. Leonard gets patches to baste onto his old clothes and a hat. He's a tramp. With a bundle on a stick. I'll help him."

Ethel walked out of the room without a word. Mrs. Mack watched her leave. She said, "I wish they'd ask that girl to the party. She's a lonesome thing." She sighed. "Maybe next year they will. Now what did you need that basket for?"

I couldn't wait to tell Bella what I'd learned. "And you were right. Everyone knows where we live. I feel so stupid. I'm such a dummy." I took a deep breath. "But the costume turned out all right. Mrs. Mack is giving me empty packages to fill the basket and a cloth napkin to cover it. I'll look like I'm bringing goodies to my grandma."

"Your grandma's back in New York."

"In the story, Silly. You know. Well, I'll be the only Little Red Riding Hood at the party, but there will be lots of tramps and ghosts I suppose."

"Now will you write your address on the RSVP envelope?"

I smiled. "Don't know why she wants it in the mail. Maybe I should write one and hand it to her at school."

"No no no. She'll love getting it in the mail. Let me help you write one."

"With your scribble scrabble? No thank you."

Milwaukee Building Co
Architectural Designers
NEW BVILDINGS OF
THE JEWISH ORPHANS HOME OF SOVTHERN CALIFORNIA
BEING ERECTED AT THE S.E. CORNER OF MILES & IRVINGTON AVES. - HVNTINGTON PARK-CAL.

Dedication Day

Fresh Eggs!

Children at Play, Huntington Park

One of the Cottages at Huntington Park

Eastlake Park

Thanksgiving Dinner at
A. L. Levy's Restaurant
November 24, 1910

Dr. Sigmund Frey

Chapter 9

BOYS, HALLOWEEN, CANDY, CHANNUKAH

I whispered in my softest voice, "Wake up, Bella."

She turned over in her sleep.

I put my mouth to her ear. "Wake up and don't make any noise."

She yawned, opened her eyes. Her sleepy eyes grew wider after she spotted my eyes looking into hers. Even though it was dark in the dorm we could make out each other's shadowy, bulky shapes. "Sh. I brought you some candy. Here. Here's your favorite. A Tootsie Roll. I took one of the candies from my basket and unwrapped it. She yawned again and I popped it into her mouth.

"I brushed my teeth." She sat up and chewed. "I'm not going back to brush again."

"Quiet." I looked around. Some of the girls in the dorm shifted in their beds, but none seemed to wake up.

"The party was great." I handed her another candy.

My raincoat lay spread out on my bed where I'd tossed it after I snuck real quiet upstairs. "They thought Little Red Riding Hood was great and I used my basket to gather up enough candy for both of us. From their backyard treasure hunt."

Bella finished her candy and lay back down.

"They played John Brown's Body. That's where this John Brown died a horrible death and they dug up his body. They passed around his parts." I whispered closer to her ear. "First they passed around a peeled grape."

"Uh huh."

"That was supposed to be his eye. Oh, I forgot to tell you. We were blindfolded."

"Oh." She rolled over on her tummy.

"And a real piece of raw liver on a plate. That was supposed to be his liver. We peeked at it. It was icky."

"Bella." I pushed at her shoulder.

She moaned. "What?"

I looked around. Some of the girls were stirring. Beds creaked.

I whispered, "I'll tell you tomorrow. Go back to sleep."

The dorm was very dark and quiet now. I slipped the basket full of candy under my bed. My red skirt, wrinkled and dirty, clung to my legs. I changed into my nightgown in the alcove. But I didn't get under the covers right away. First I reached into the basket under the bed. I gathered up two big handfuls of candy. The room was still quiet except for occasional light breathing sounds. I stayed very still for a few minutes.

Ethel's bed stood far from mine. So I had to walk on tiptoe not to wake anyone. I reached her bed and bent down. I placed the candies in a pile under her bed, listened to make sure that everyone still slept.

In the morning no one noticed anything. I waited till all the girls made their beds and clattered down the stairs to breakfast. Even Bella trotted along with them, and she hadn't said anything about last night.

I got out my basket, still full of candy. Last night was such fun. Everyone at Helen's party, not just me, filled little bags with suckers, hard candies, peppermints, toffee and Tootsie Rolls. I got to gather more because I had my basket with me, and only one boy said, "Hey, that's not fair." The others laughed. They teased me and called me

Little Red. I laughed along with them.

I'd walked home in the dark with Leonard and Abraham, gave them candies from my basket to add to their own bags.

"Thanks, Celia. You're an angel. Ha ha." Abraham nudged Leonard. Leonard pushed him away.

He said, "Helen was the angel. All in white like that."

"Yes.," I laughed with them. "Her mother made her costume. Even that halo."

"Too bad it got torn off her head."

"She didn't care."

"Watch where you're going."

They bumped into each other, walked crazy. We got close to the entrance to the Home.

Mrs. Mack met us at the gate and told us to be quiet because it was so late. Everyone had gone to bed a long time ago. I grinned to myself when I heard her tsk tsk under her breath because no grownup had walked us home.

At breakfast maybe Mrs. Mack thought I slept late because I got home late. But I woke up at the usual time. I delayed getting dressed. Since no one was in the dorm to watch me I walked briskly up and down, placing candies on all the pillows until the basket was almost empty. Then I emptied the last little unwrapped chocolate drops into my clothes drawer.

I swung the empty basket back and forth on my way down the stairs.

"Where've you been?" someone asked. "You're late," another girl said. A big chorus of girls with questions fell on me. I handed the basket to Mrs. Mack and sat down at my place.

"Celia's got a sweetheart," a girl named Rachel-Ann said. The others joined in. "Celia, Celia pudding and pie, got a sweetheart that's no lie."

"What are you talking about?" Burning salt tears filled my eyes, but they didn't spill out, probably because I was so mad.

"Someone saw you holding hands with Leonard last night."

"I did not! Who said that?"

"Some one who helped bring in the eggs this morning. They said so."

"Who?"

"Girls. Stop talking and finish eating." Mrs. Mack trundled up to the front of our tables. "It's time to bring in your plates."

Everyone looked away from me and quieted down, but Ethel. She stared at me.

If she only knew I'd given her candy. Bella moved her plate closer to mine on the table. She clinked her fork against mine to get my attention. There was a soft murmur in the room as girls began talking again. Some got up to take their plates away.

"Celia, last night you woke me up."

"I thought you didn't remember."

"I did. I found Tootsie Roll spots on the collar of my nightie. I remembered. But I didn't want the other girls to hear me ask you about it. Wasn't it a secret?"

"That's okay. I gave them all candy, too. I put some on their beds. Let's see if they notice when they get up to get ready for school."

"You started to tell me about the party but I think I fell asleep."

"I'll tell you more later."

"Is it true that Leonard is your sweetheart?"

"No! They're crazy. I just walked with him, that's all. You were right, Bella. I should have listened to you. Remember when you knew all their names? And I didn't? You told me then that I never pay attention."

"Well, I never see you talking to them."

"Maybe I will now. Leonard and Abraham were nice. But listen. I don't have any sweetheart."

"Celia!" Rachel-Ann and some of the other girls ran down from upstairs and into the dining room. "Celia. Did you give us this candy?"

"Happy Halloween. It's a holiday."

"Girls." Mrs. Mack raised her voice. "Don't eat candy now. Better you should wait till after supper. It's too early."

Too late. They all munched on their candy.

I got up to put my dish away. Oh, no. Here comes Ethel. She blocked my way.

"I found a bunch of candy under my bed."
"Sorry if I made a mess."
"So it was you put it there?"
"I thought you'd like it."
She nodded.
I nodded back, took my dishes into the kitchen.
Bella followed me, held me back to talk to me. "Celia, I can't believe you gave extra candy to that girl. She's never nice to you."
"I feel bad for her."
"Maybe Ethel's class did what mine did yesterday."
"What's that?"
"We cut out black cats and pumpkins and had our own party in school."
"Yeah, we did, too."
"So Ethel had a party at school and you don't have to feel bad for her."
I decided then not to tell Bella the rest of what we did at Helen's party. The costume prizes, the decorations, the Jack 'o lantern cookies and pumpkin pies. Her class party would have been enough.

Chanukah

In November Mama wrote me again that she was getting better. I sighed, added her letter to my stack, all tied together under a pretty purple ribbon. I didn't even mention it to Bella. She always told me that Mama was getting better, and I let her think she'd be well soon. I myself didn't believe it would be soon.

In December our rabbi told us we were going to have a Chanukah party. We all loved the story of how the Jews stayed in their temple with not enough oil to burn to have light. A miracle happened and the tiny amount of oil lasted eight days. The Maccabees were great warriors and won battles, and that was miraculous, too.

But just learning bible stories was not as exciting as this party was going to be. The festivities were to be held in the synagogue on the eighth night. Every night before that we went to the front of the room and gathered around the candelabra, our menorah. The rabbi held up the littlest child to light one candle.

On the third day it was still early evening when I stayed out on the grounds searching among the dying plants in my garden patch.

"Hey, Celia. Look up."

"What?"

I couldn't see much because twilight dimmed the air. I looked back at Leonard. His blond wavy hair came down low behind his ears. His face was narrow and long, but his eyes were round and smiley. His overalls looked cleaner than most of the boys when they worked in the garden.

"Where's the sun?" he asked.

"It's going down." I turned and squinted. "It's mostly behind the shed."

"You know what that means, don't you?"

"What?" I looked back down at my plot. Most of the plants had turned brown and dry. A few small vegetables still hid under drying leaves. Those were what I'd been trying to search out.

"It's sundown, remember?"

'Oh my gosh." Now I looked up and all around the grounds. No one was there but me and Leonard.

"We're going to be late."

He jumped over a small stake leaning against a dead corn stalk.

"Come on." He ran toward the main building.

I stuck out the toe of my shoe to smooth down the dirt around the plant I'd been planning to dig up.

"Let's go" he called after me.

I started after him, but slowly. He slowed his pace to keep back with me.

No! I wanted him to go ahead. There'd be too much teasing if we went in together.

After last Halloween whenever we walked home from school at the same time I made sure I was in a group with Abraham and some others. Never alone with Leonard. The earlier teasing had died down and I didn't want any more like that.

Kids were still filing in from their cottages and the dorm. No one paid attention to what time I arrived up in the synagogue. I found Bella and stood with her in the crowd of children around the table with the menorah.

They'd pushed the chairs that we sat on during Friday services to the walls. That made room for us all to cluster around the candelabra. Someone had covered the table with a white cloth that had filament-thin gold colored stripes. The large silver candelabra had all kinds of designs etched into it and what looked like welded-on decorations in gold colored metal. Two of the white candles already burned, along with the higher-up middle one. That was the Shamus, the caretaker one.

"Celia, I think those two are still lit from the night before,"Bella said.

"They wouldn't last that long," Leonard said. He found me in that group, heard what Bella told me.

She looked up at him. "How do you know?"

"I'm going to be a scientist. I study those things."

"But they were lighted up when I walked in here just now."

"They must have put new ones in. Right, Celia?"

"I guess so." I walked farther away from them.

He followed me. "Remember how I asked you where the sun was? That's because I'm studying astronomy."

Bella laughed. "Come on, Leonard. They don't have a class of that at our school."Everybody was listening to them. I tried to look like I wasn't with them.

"You don't have to study a subject in school. I talk about it with our Sloyd teacher. He knows all about the subject. And I have books."

Bella planted her hands on her hips. "Books about candles or books about the sun?"

Leonard didn't seem to notice how everyone smiled at him. I walked farther away.

"You don't know everything." Bella lifted her arm up to his head. A black yarmulke, a skullcap, covered the back of his blond hair. She grabbed it off and put it on her own head.

Now I really wanted to drop through the floor. Both of them. So embarrassing.

The rabbi heard a bunch of laughter. He came over from where he'd stood at the side talking with Mrs. Mack.

Bella must have known she shouldn't have done that. When the Rabbi came over she took it off her own head and handed it to him.

"Who does this belong to, My Dear."

"Him. Leonard."

The rabbi placed it on Leonard's head. He adjusted it and said. "Very nice."

A different type of black hat covered the rabbi's head. Its wide brim stood up around a high crown. His beard was black and neatly trimmed, but he had thick, black hair hanging down behind his ears.

"Rabbi." Bella faced him." Why can't girls wear Yarmulkes? We say the prayers, too."

"Well, in the old country the women put scarves on their heads. Would you like that dear? We can find a pretty white lace cap for you."

"No, that's okay. I like the ones the boys have. That's all. They're round. And they keep their hair in order."

Leonard glared at her. "That's not their purpose."

"Your hair is very nice the way it is." The rabbi patted Bella on the head.

Mrs. Mack had a white piece of cloth pinned on the back of her hair with a hairpin. But nobody seemed to notice that. It looked like a handkerchief to me.

"Who is going to light the third candle tonight?" The Rabbi's voice got loud. We all stood in silence.

"Who will it be?" He picked up the middle candle, the Shamus.

We all looked at one another. No one volunteered. I noticed that Bella was focused on one of those boys I remembered her talking to by the woodshop. That was the time she informed me that she knew all their names. This boy was shorter than her but she'd told me he was older. He looked like one of the youngest. But he wasn't. He stayed in the cottage where the younger boys slept.

Uh oh. What was Bella going to do next? Sure enough she

pushed through the kids near her and stopped by this Julius. "You," she whispered to him. He was startled, moved his head toward her, his mouth open.

Of course the rabbi saw the movement and handed him the candle.

"Do you know the prayer?"

Julius shrugged.

"Yes, he does. We all do" Bella told the rabbi.

I didn't know whether I was more embarrassed by her butting in like that or more proud that we all had studied well and we knew the Hebrew so well.

That night back in the dorm I practically shouted at Bella. "We only have four more days to light candles before the party. Can you keep your mouth shut until then? Please?"

The synagogue was fitted out with long rows of tables on the night of our Chanukah party. The ladies of the Benevolent Society had come and set everything up. Dr. Frey led us in our Hebrew chanting and the lighting ceremony.

"Line up, Children."

We were supposed to stand in rows to sing the songs we'd rehearsed last week. Nobody pushed and shoved like they did when we were learning it.

Chanukah lights are shining brightly
Over the world this wintry night
And our hearts are ever grateful
As we light the Chanukah lights

"Such joy you give us, Children. How beautiful. Like angels you sounded."

"Come up here, Alice." Dr. Frey smiled so wide his mustache turned up higher than usual on the ends.

He gave Alice the *Shamus* to light the last of the eight candles, symbolizing the miracle of the lights. She looked beautiful in a long slim skirt and a cream colored blouse with flowing sleeves. Carved ivory combs held up her smooth, straight hair.

She said she was honored. I was sad because I knew it would be her last time.

Dr. Frey made a nice speech for us all. At the end he held up the menorah.

"Children, young ones, look at this for more than what it symbolizes. It is a treasure that I brought to this country wrapped in layers of linen. This came from my homeland in Europe, from an old and ancient tradition. We Jews have kept our traditions alive for centuries. We honor the past and now you represent the future."

He spoke more about our lives ahead, but all I could concentrate on was watching Bella. She seemed to be having trouble keeping herself from giggling. I wanted to smack her. Maybe I could step on her shoes. No, then she'd scream ow. What was he saying now?

He thanked the Benevolent Society for the party. They'd brought us all gifts. We lined up and walked past them so they could hand us each a package to unwrap. We all got stockings and underwear and different books and a gold coin each.

I rubbed my coin in my palm with my fingers and it was real shiny. Everybody held up their coins to read the inscription. I saw a menorah on mine.

Dr. Frey cleared his throat. "Children, *Kinder*, these coins are called Chanukah *gelt*. When the Maccabees won the battle, the vanquished king said: 'I turn over to you the right to make your own stamp for coinage for your country.'"

Finally we could sit down to our meal. The ladies helped the cook bring up steaming platters of *latkes*, potato pancakes fried in oil. Dr Frey wasn't through with his speech making. Now he told us in his loud voice that the oil the *latkes* were cooked in symbolized the oil that burned for eight days in the temple.

Bella sat next to me. "Our mama makes excellent latkes, Celia. Remember?"

"How can I forget? I used to help her grate the potatoes."

"Next year we'll be back in our house and you can grate them again."

"You better help me. You're old enough now."

I said that to her. But didn't really know if it was to be that way or not. The chicken and the rest of the food didn't taste as good as Mama's cooking, either.

Chapter 10

ANOTHER FUNERAL

"This time I'm sure Mama will come and get us very soon." Bella waved her letter in front of my eyes.

I stood up from the bed where I'd stretched out to read my own letter. "This time I think you're right." I grabbed her and we danced around in a little circle hugging each other.

Rachel-Ann looked over at us. She set down her hairbrush and shook out her curls. "What are you two so happy about?"

"It's my mom. She wrote that the doctor said she's almost well."

"What's sputum?" Bella interrupted us.

"That's spit. The doctor said it's been clear for a while."

"Rachel-Ann said, "I guess you'll be able to go home then. Just when I got to be your friend, Celia. Oh well. I'll be happy for you."

"Don't be so fast. Last time she visited us it turned out she had clear sputum then, too. But the blood came back after that."

Bella said "So our mom had to go back in the sanatorium again. But this time I'm sure it's gone for good."

Rachel-Ann and I both smiled down on Bella, like she was our little pet. "Yes, Sweetheart. We'd better head down for dinner." I looked around the dorm. Most of the girls were already downstairs. We followed after them.

This letter with the doctor's good comments was why I looked forward to the next Sunday. Maybe Mama would visit us. That's why I wasn't scared the very next day when Dr. Frey sent for me to come to his office. I skipped and grinned and made my way across the marble floor to his door. I tapped and opened it.

Dr. Frey got up from his desk. He motioned me to a chair and then, very strangely, he sat on the chair beside me. He put his arm around my shoulder.

"Celia, dear."

This wasn't good.

"I have to tell you some very bad news."

"Is t…? I barely got out the words. "Is it about my mother?"

"No. It's your brother."

"Sam?"

"No. Avrum. The one they call Abraham."

I stared at his shiny black telephone that hung from the wall behind his desk. "Is he sick?"

"Well, he was sick. He was in the hospital for a few days but I'm so sorry to have to tell you…" He looked me in the eye, tightened his arm around me. "The doctors weren't able to save him. Your mother wants you to be strong." He nodded his head at me.

"Abraham?" I didn't believe him. "Did he cough blood, too?" My voice was high and soft.

"No, no. He didn't contract tuberculosis. He got appendicitis. A burst appendix."

"Bella won't believe you. She needs him. He's her special brother." I put my fist to my eyes. "He's my special brother, too. He's the nice one, he's the one Mama relies on, it can't be." I said that all at once. Then I stopped. The lump in my throat would not let me say another word. I stared at the floor.

"It's hard. I know. Tomorrow, Sunday is the funeral. Your brother Sam will come for you in his wagon. He will take you to your mother and then to the funeral. But I have a message. Your mother said to tell you this. She does not want you to bring Bella to the funeral."

That was what she wanted? I looked up at him, a question on my lips.

"She remembered how Bella collapsed at your dear father's

funeral. She does not want Bella to have to go through that again. She's too young." He took his arm away and got up, went back to his chair behind the dark wooden desk.

"But…but she'll know about it..."

"You can tell her afterwards."

"How can I keep it a secret? She'll know."

There was another tap at the door. Maybe it was Bella. But no. Mrs. Mack came in. She kneeled in front of me. "I'm so sorry, Celia."

"I want to go to my room now."

Dr. Frey said, "Do you think you can go through the rest of the day in your, uh, normal way? To protect your sister?"

I shrugged.

"She wants to be alone." Mrs. Mack patted my back. "Let her go."

"No," Dr. Frey said. "We can't send her out like this. He came over and took my hand. "I'll tell you what. Come for a walk with me around the campus. We'll go on an inspection of the grounds. You don't want to be with the others now, do you? A sad thing happened in your family."

I did not want to go with him. How could I tell him that? My body went limp. I couldn't grasp that Abe could be gone. He couldn't be. It wasn't right. It changed everything. Our family. The whole world.

I walked with Dr. Frey down the paths where the families visited on Sundays. When we came to the spot where Mama had last come to us, I pulled away. I ran behind a row of bushes off to the side. My bones felt like jelly. I sat on the grass. I stayed there a long time. I didn't cry. I couldn't. But I had to be alone. I hoped Dr. Frey wouldn't wait for me. But when I finally got up and came back out onto the path, he was there waiting calmly.

"Your mother wanted Bella not to know yet. Did you understand that?"

I nodded.

So let's see if you can get through the rest of the day and the morning. It has to do with a special bond your mother says she felt with Abraham."

"Uh huh. Okay. I won't say anything. I'll do what my mother

wanted." The tears started now. I wiped my face with my sleeve.

I managed to stay away from my sister the rest of the time. I saw her playing a ball game with her friends and that was good.

I fell asleep thinking of my poor mother. Wasn't it grief enough when Papa died?

In the morning I hoped I'd had a bad dream. But it wasn't. I waited upstairs after breakfast until Bella was dressed and out. Then I put on my black dress, and went to wait for Sam down near the gate.

It wasn't long before I could see him pull up the buggy just outside. He hitched the horse to the wrought iron rail. I ran down the path to meet him. I got there, turned around, and saw Bella come out of nowhere. She'd been behind a group of visitors who were off to the side.

"Sam!" she called. She ran as fast as her legs could take her. "Sam! Celia!"

Suddenly she stopped "Celia! Why are you wearing that black dress?"

I shrugged.

Sam threw his horse switch into the wagon. He walked up to the gate facing me through the bars. "Look, Celia. We have to tell her sooner or later. Tell her now. Avrum, our Abraham, died. There."

"No, I don't believe you. Now it was Bella's turn to be in disbelief. "Where are you going?"

"To his funeral," answered Sam, snarling.

"Well, I have to go, too. I have to. I'm going, too."

"But Mama said," I started to say.

Sam looked me straight in the eye. "Let her go."

Mrs. Mack had been observing from the path. She trundled on down toward us.

She panted, waved her arms. "I don't believe your mother wants her to attend."

"She's attending. He was her brother, too. I won't leave her behind," Sam said. "If she doesn't go, none of us go."

"I don't have a black dress," said Bella. She held out her skirts and cried. Her tears came for her dress, but I knew it was really for the death.

"You're wearing a brown one. That's good enough," said Sam. "Get up in the buggy."

We both ran out the gate and climbed up. Sam waved goodbye to Mrs. Mack. I hunkered down on the seat, afraid to look back at her. But Bella waved, so I turned around in time to see a helpless look on Mrs. Mack's face. We drove away.

The sky looked cloudy and the air felt cold. Cypress bushes along the route bent in the wind. Like the day Papa died. Again I wondered if it's always gloomy like this when someone dies. No, that would be silly. But still it seemed that way

Sam followed Pacific Boulevard toward the bridge over the Los Angeles River. None of us said anything. Finally I broke our silence. "How long have you known, Sam?"

"Since they took him away to the hospital three days ago. They wouldn't let me in to see him."

The road was bumpy with puddles from a recent rain. The cart lurched. Sam stood up in the driver's seat. He raised his hand toward the heavens. He shook his fist at the sky. "God damn you, God! God Damn you, God!"

"SAM!" I put my hands over my mouth. "You better not talk that way."

"Why not? Do you think God will punish me?" He laughed a horrible sounding laugh.

"It's not right."

"Oh, no? Our prayers tell us to thank God when things go right. So, shouldn't we also get to blame God when he takes away your brother? And your father?"

He sat back down. Bella reached for his arm. "Listen, Sammy," she said. "The rabbi said everything happens for a reason."

"What was the reason Abe died? What was the reason Papa died? So we could suffer? Good reason, Bella."

She put her finger in her mouth. Her eyebrows came together as she thought hard. "Sam. Maybe you're right. There was no reason." She stood up on the wooden floorboards, and in her small voice, imitated Sam. "God damn you, God!" She shook her fist toward heaven, like he did.

"Bella!" I couldn't believe what I heard. "You mustn't swear."

"Okay, Celia." She shook both fists upwards. "Darn you, God!"

"Sit down." I almost laughed. That wasn't what I'd meant. I stroked her hair.

"Abraham was the best of all of us," Sam said.

"He was the best." Bella cried for the first time. "I loved him so much."

Sam stopped the cart in front of our neighbor's house. My eyes were so full of water that I almost didn't notice that this was not our house. Our house looked so wonderful. Our old house. A long time ago. Then I saw Sam unhitch Blackie and lead him down our neighbor's path toward their next-door stable.

"Sam. Where are you going?"

"Stay there. We had to sell Blackie. But you can visit him. The neighbors let us see him. I clean their stable, too. You can feed him sugar cubes. But not now. Stay in the wagon a minute."

Bella and I stared at each other. "Papa's horsy," she said.

"What about the vegetable route that Uncle took over from Papa?" I called after Sam.

"They went back to New York." Sam led Blackie on by his reins.

This was a lot of news to take in.

Sam came back and helped me down. "Stay there, Bellie. I want to tell Mama you're here with us first."

It wasn't like her to sit still, but she folded her hands on her lap, nodded, and stared straight ahead.

Bella was almost eight years old now, and I was had just turned eleven.

I clung on to my brother Sam's hand as he led me up the steps. Out of the corner of my eye I spotted the brilliant white blossoms of the hydrangea bush alongside our porch. Those flowers would be the last bright color I'd see for a long time. We opened the door to darkness and silence

My mother sat in a chair against the wall, her skirts spread in folds over her legs. Her black hair, parted in the middle, was pulled back in such a severe looking bun that not one loose hair softened her face. Her dark eyes were ringed in red. I stepped on tiptoe toward her, then ran to her, knelt down and threw my head in her lap. Her arms surrounded me.

"Mama," I sighed a long slow breath. At last.

After our long hug she looked up at Sam. He'd grown tall, looked so dressed up in a black jacket and black long pants. His hair still combed, parted on the side, stayed in place from the morning. What kept him from looking picture perfect was the sorrow shown deep in the lines of his face.

"What is it, Sammy?"

"We brought Bella. I know you said not to, but…"

Mama stood up so fast I got pushed to the side. "Where is she?" Mama burst out the front door. She ran down the steps.

I watched Mama from the doorway reach up to Bella on the seat. Bella stayed as still as when Sam told her to stay. But Mama grasped her around the waist, pulled her down, and brought her inside. The three of us clung together and cried and cried.

"They're here, Mama." Sam tapped her arms; she was hugging us forever.

"It's the hearse to take us to the cemetery."

"So soon? No time, a glass of water, a bite to eat, for my *maidlach*, my girls?"

The driver knocked on the door.

Mama sighed, locked up the empty house. The four of us got in the ugly black car with the driver, who held his hat in one hand while helping us in. We drove, looked out the windows.

So much like when Papa died. But so different, too.

At the gravesite our family sat in chairs. The rabbi motioned the other mourners to wait for him to begin. This time when Bella and I looked at the deep hole in the ground and the mound of dark earth, we knew what to expect. Mama held extra tight to Bella's hand. We all knew why.

I looked around to see people in black clothes, but not nearly as many as had come to Papa's funeral. Mrs. Matlin came over and hugged me. Others told us their condolences. The rabbi's talk began with how sad for all of us when a child dies. He didn't have to tell us. As if we didn't know. He said nice things about Abraham, or Avrum, the way his Hebrew name would be written on the gravestone. I wondered if he really knew him or if he heard people say what a helpful good good boy Abraham always was—peacemaker, a good student, a hard worker, a loving brother, a loving son.

Some lady came by our row and passed out a bunch of clean hankies. Our tears wet them all and we could have used a few more.

Bella didn't collapse, but it seemed that Mama was about to. Two men held her up after the shoveling of dirt on the grave.

One of the men drove us home in a smaller black car than the one we came in.

Our house did not look as empty and scary when we got home as it had before the funeral. Mama's friend Mrs. Matlin came to help. She and some other women did what Tante Becky had done last year. They brought platters of tasty, traditional food.

Gracie's mother came with a casserole. Behind her, hanging back, I saw Gracie. Bella went to her. She took her hand. "Hi, Gracie."

The two girls walked hand in hand into the back yard.

So many of the grown-ups bent down to tell me how sorry they were. I guess last year I was too young. Only a year ago none of them paid much attention to us kids. This year everyone wanted us to know how bad they felt.

Mr. Raphael knelt down and talked to me in his kind, nasal twang,

"How are they treating you in the Jewish Home, Celia?"

"They're nice."

"Do you get enough to eat?"

"Yes."

"Do you get enough playtime?"

"Yes."

"In school, are you learning?"

"Yes."

"That's it?" It was like he wanted me to say more. But I had nothing to say. He smiled at me, shook his head. He got up to talk to another friend of Papa's. Mr. Raphael was really a nice man, but I didn't have anything to say to him. Or to anyone.

"Have some chopped liver, a sandwich, Celia." Mrs. Matlin led me to the table. Her older daughter came with her baby. People made a fuss over the baby. A lady with screwed-up lips and frowning eyebrows told another lady in a navy blue dress that she didn't think it right to have a baby at a house of mourning. That lady shrugged, looked away, made herself a pickled herring platter.

Our windows had black coverings like before and the room was still dark. But the people were talking in groups, not mourning sounding at all.

"Sam. What are you doing?" I found him leaning in a doorway.

"Nothing."

I whispered," Some of Papa's friends act like they're at a party."

"Some of them haven't seen each other for a year. Or Mama either. She was away, you remember."

"But Abraham was …"

"I know. Let's go out."

We sat on the front steps.

"Why did Tante and Uncle go back? Did they miss New York so much? Did Isaac not make friends here?"

"Uncle felt guilty. He kept telling everyone if only he hadn't brought such a heavy trunk. If only Louis had let him carry it himself. If only Louis had not had to step on the platform so hard."

"So did you think it was his fault? Did Mama think so?"

"No. No. That's not it. Just bad luck. Damn rotten luck." Sam ran his hand along the flat railing. "Are you going to tell me not to swear again?"

"No." I leaned my face in my palms. I took a deep breath. "Sam. Remember what you were saying before? About God?"

His mouth turned halfway up in one corner. "Yeah."

"I think God is like Santa Claus."

"Why is that?"

"What I mean is that there is no Santa Claus. Not really. He exists only in stories. And I think it's the same with God."

The screen door slammed. Gracie's mom came out of the house. She'd wrapped her empty casserole dish in white cloth. Bella and Gracie came walking around from the back. We heard loud conversations from in the house until Gracie's mom shut the front door.

She acted all flustered, looked at us like she was searching for words to comfort us, but couldn't find any. She said, "We have to go home. Gracie, give your friend a nice goodbye. Bella has to go back tonight. You can play again when they come back home."

The thought of leaving made my throat choke up tight. I was glad that Bella didn't look sad now. Gracie's mom said to me, "Don't worry, Celia. Your mother is on the road to recovery. We'll see you back here before you know it."

We watched them walk up the sidewalk. Gracie turned around to Bella and waved every so often, and Bella waved her little hand in a quiet sort of way.

But when they were gone from sight she asked Sam, "What were you talking about?"

"Celia told me God's like Santa Claus."

"Does God come down the chimney for good Christian children on Christmas night?" She laughed. She knew that wasn't what I meant.

"In stories, I meant. He's in stories. Like those exciting bible stores that we read. And, Sam, you know how you said if you can thank God for good things, then why can't you also blame God for bad things?"

He nodded.

I inhaled the air around us, damp, clean Los Angeles air. "I don't think there's any reason to thank god or blame god at all."

Bella scratched her head. "What are you talking about? I don't get it."

Sam ignored her. He spoke to me. "So you don't blame god for Papa or for Abe or for anything."

"No, why should we? Because if god's only in stories, but not real, what's the point?"

"Then why'd you get so upset when I cursed yesterday?"

"I kept thinking about that during the funeral. Those curse words.

Nobody heard them but us. Because there's nobody up in heaven listening. Not if you say a million prayers. And this is the other part. Not if you say a million bad, evil cursing things, either. Who cares?"

"Yeah, but..." said Bella. "But why should I keep trying to be a good girl if there is no God looking down on me?"

"Because you should. And I didn't think you were listening to me and Sam. So butt out."

"Let her listen. She's not so little any more. But she probably thinks she'll see Abe and Papa up in heaven."

"Yes, I will. I know I will."

"That's what they all think. I'd love to see Abraham. Just one more time. I needed to tell him something." Sam choked up, stopping himself from crying.

"What, Sammy?" I rubbed his back.

"That it wasn't the loquat seeds."

"What are you talking about?"

"He thought he got sick because he ...he swallowed all the seeds. But it wasn't that. I swallowed seeds, too. He just ate too much of...of"

Sammy broke down and cried. He sobbed out, "He didn't need to blame the loquat tree. I'm the one. The one who showed him where the tree grew, how full and yellow gold, plump fruit all bunched up on branches there for us to pick."

Bella and I took each other's hands. The sight of our big older brother so broken up gave us goose bumps.

Chapter 11

Second Summer at the Home, New Clothes

"Can I have a needle and thread, Mrs. Mack?"

"Celia, what are you doing here? I thought you were on the playground with the others." Mrs. Mack turned around from the wall with all the shelves. She stopped straightening the toys and books in the children's reading room.

"I was. But I came in just now."

"What do you need a needle and thread for?"

"I want to take down the hem on Bella's dress. She's grown so much. You can see her legs above her knees."

"That's not so good. Let me get you the thread. What color? And you'll need scissors."

"Dark blue, I guess."

"Stand still. Let me see you. Oh, you've grown, too. Your dress could use some lengthening."

"That's okay. They're wearing them short now. You should see the girls at school. But not as short as Bella's."

"Lift your arm up."

I did, felt funny, don't know why.

"Isn't it tight on you?"

"A little."

"Come with me." She opened a cupboard where they kept the

yarn for knitting and the embroidery materials. She handed me a little sewing kit.

"I wish your mother was better. I'd ask her to send you new clothes." She sighed.

I didn't answer her. I didn't want to think about how Mama was right now. An awful scene took place when we left to come back here. When Dr. Frey sent a car to bring Bella and me back to the Home Mother held on to me and Bella with all her might. She cried out, "*Mine kinderlach*, my babies, my children."

Sammy and the neighbors had to pull her hands off of us. Mrs. Matlin tired to calm her. "They'll be back. Soon, Esther. You'll be together again soon. You need to rest now. Come, lie down."

The friends who gathered around in the living room gave us pitying looks, between their mouthfuls of food. I held my head down low. Bella tried holding on to Mama, but Sammy had to pry her hands off and take her out down the front steps. I followed, trying to shrink myself.

I did not know if Mrs. Mack had heard about that.

"You do need new clothes, Celia. I'll talk to the Society."

"It's crooked, Celia. My dress on the bottom. You made it crooked." Bella twirled around.

"I did the best I could. Wait." I hitched up her waist. "There. Look in the mirror. It's good now."

"Okay. It's good enough."

She didn't really care how she looked. She cared about being on a winning team when her class played ball, that's all.

I cared. That's why I copied Helen and Rachel-Ann. In summer school they combined the grades. That's why my two friends became friends with each other. We were all in the same art class this summer.

We stood in front of the long mirror in the girls' bathroom.

"How'd you get your hair into such nice curls, Helen?" Rachel-Ann primped her own naturally curly hair.

"I used rags. Do you know how to make rag curls, Celia? I'll show you."

The three of us patted our hair, pinched our cheeks for color, smoothed down the collars of our dresses. We walked out onto the bright playground.

Summer was at its height now. The trees edging our wire fence bent from loads of grass-green leaves. Weighted-down branches tilted toward the ground. Some drooped over the top of the fence. Clusters of dropped leaves covered much of the dirt edging. We walked toward the fence, talking, laughing, enjoying being girls together. Stepping on the green leaves squished them, but didn't crunch like brown ones in the fall.

"There's that kid over there who lives at your place," Helen said.

I had to look twice to see three boys slouching by a tetherball pole.

Rachel-Ann was quick to answer. She said, "Yes. That one's Leonard. I think he likes Celia, and the good looking one is Donald. But he doesn't live at our place. The other one, Abraham, does. Him and his brother Julius."

"I know Donald," Helen said. "And Abraham's my brother's friend. "Why don't we go talk to them." She started off. Rachel-Ann kept up with her. I trailed along.

"Hi. What're you doing?' Helen said.

"Nothing."

Abraham pointed to the road just beyond the fence. "Look at all them cars. I think there's more of them than the carriages."

That made me wonder how Blackie was doing back at our neighbors.

"I'm going to get me one as soon as I get out of here."

"Yeah. Me, too." Donald spit. I wondered why boys did that.

Leonard turned toward me. "Celia, look where the sun is. Did you know you can tell time by the sun? It must be noon because the sun's right up overhead."

I shrugged. Rachel-Ann asked. "You're only interested in scientist stuff? Aren't you going to get a car, too?"

"Sure I want one. Just that when Celia was in the garden that day we talked about the sun going down in the west and..."

"I don't remember that," I managed to say.

The other boys didn't catch that. They talked to each other about the different kinds of cars, model T's, Doosies, and French models, and what they would choose. But the girls had different reactions.

Helen first. She said, "Celia, you and Leonard in the garden together. Rachel-Ann, did you see them there?"

"Not me. They must have been hiding there."

"Oh, in your home can you do that?"

"You'd be surprised at what we can do. In secret."

"That's stupid" I said. "They're always looking at us. We can never be alone. I gotta go. The bell's gonna ring."

"Celia's got a boyfriend, Celia's got….."

"Drop it." I gave Helen the meanest look I knew how to make.

"Okay." She got the message. "So what kind of a car do you want, Rachel-Ann? Or can't girls have cars?"

"Sure we can," I heard Rachel-Ann tell Helen. I strode off toward the buildings.

That night I searched in all my drawers and Bella's. I was looking for the most worn-out item of clothing we had. I settled on one of Bella's undershirts.

I sat on my bed and spread it out over my knees. I cut through the hemming with my manicure scissors. Then I tore it into strips. Some came out ragged but others looked straight enough. Bella came into the room.

"Hey. That's mine. What are you doing?"

"Well, it used to be mine. It's a hand-me-down. And you'll never get more use out of it."

Now Rachel-Ann came in. "Oh, I know what she's doing."

I picked up my comb.

"She wants to have curls like me." Rachel-Ann fluffed her curls, so proud of her hair.

Our other roommates came and watched. I wrapped sections of my hair in tight spirals with the rags, then tied them with knots.

Ethel stood there, watched me like a hawk.

I said, "What am I, a free show? Go to bed."

The others reached their hands up to their own hair, some straight, some thick, some wavy, then wandered off. Ethel stayed. I kept wrapping until all my hair was covered in rags.

"You look like a mop," Ethel told me.

"Your head looks like a coconut with banana peels waving over it." Bella said.

Before I could scream at them Bella felt my head. "Will you be able to sleep like that, Celia?"

"Of course." I got into bed, put the covers over my head. I fell asleep right away, before I had a chance to worry about what Ethel said, or about what my friends at school said about Leonard earlier in the day.

When I woke up the next morning I gave a fierce frown at the girls, even Bella. No one dared to stand over me and watch. I untied all the rags, went to look in the mirror.

Oh, no! I looked like a topsy turvy kind of person, with curls all right. But the curls stuck up all over my head in every direction. I rushed to the sink and wet my hair. I combed it. It looked nice when I got the curls to stay at the bottom. But I was too embarrassed to let them stay. I wet and combed until my hair looked straight again.

One of the girls laughed at me. But Rachel-Ann came over and said, "You should have left the curls in when they were combed down."

I shook my head. Drops of water dripped on my shoulders.

"Maybe you'll try again another day."

She linked her arm in mine when we started off to school that day.

On Saturday Mrs. Mack had us all line up in the dining room.

"What's going on?" Bella asked me. I didn't have any idea. We heard noises from the entry. Mrs. Mack stood in the doorway, held out her arm to shake hands.

In came the ladies from the Benevolent Society. One wore a fur coat. In summer? Another had a fox tail wrapped around her neck. All of them wore hats, some with veils. Most wore tailored suits.

"Hello, girls. We've brought you a dressmaker," the one in furs said. She acted like the leader. She wore dangling crystal earrings and a straight black skirt under her jacket. "Let's get the tallest girl up here on the chair. "Yes, even you, Alice."

We could tell by the way Alice acted around her that she knew this lady.

The fur lady motioned to the dressmaker with her pins and measuring tapes to come closer. Starting with Alice we all got measured for new clothes.

When my turn came the lady watched the dressmaker place the tape at the back of my neck. Suddenly turning around, she put her face next to mine. "Aren't you Mrs. Heuer's daughter?"

"Yes, I am.

"I'm sorry about your mother, dear."

I was supposed to stand still for the measurements. Now I certainly would, because her words froze me in place. I couldn't even ask her what she meant by that.

Later that day I waited for a time when no one watched. I went inside and found Mrs. Mack.

"The lady from the Benevolent Society told she was sorry about my mother," I said. I waited a few minutes. Mrs. Mack had to tell me. I gulped. "Did my mother die?"

"No, Darling. Not at all. Don't you think we would have told you?"

"I don't know. Mama didn't want Bella at the funeral."

"No, no no."

"Then what did she mean?"

"Your mother had to go back into the sanatorium, that's all."

"Her coughing blood came back?"

"No." Mrs. Mack took my hands in hers.

"It's just that she's suffering from melancholia. With all the sadness, she was too incapacitated. That means she wasn't able to take care of the house, of your other brother."

"Oh," I nodded. Poor Mama. "Will she get better?"

"Yes, dear. The sanatorium is for if a person is suffering from nerves, too."

"Okay." I'd heard of nervous breakdowns. Maybe that was what Mama had.

"Did my mother have a nervous breakdown?"

"How do you know from such things? A little girl like you."

"I just know."

"She has her sickness, too, of course. Celia, aren't you excited about the new clothes you're getting? Your mother would be happy about that for you."

"Yes, Mrs. Mack."

We had to wait a week until our new clothes got sewn.

The boys all got new shoes and boots besides shirts.

We girls each got a pretty dress and a blouse and skirt, the new fashion. I got a pale yellow full skirt with a matching long sleeved blouse with ruffles at the neck and cuffs. And I got a rose-colored school dress with a white lace collar. They gave Bella a dress of a coarse material with blue and red plaid squares. She got another dress of navy blue, also with a white lace collar.

None of the girls seemed disappointed with their gifts. Just one of the littler girls said she wished her skirt was shorter. Rachel-Ann asked, "Do you think there's too much lace at my neck?" No one thought so.

Lots of changes came at the end of this summer. They needed the dorm upstairs to enlarge the synagogue and make more room for activities. A brand new cottage was built for us girls, and the boys' two cottages were joined together.

We got to go on trips, we got lessons in managing budgets, morality, what Dr. Frey called "firmness of character," and gratefulness, and cleanliness and stuff like that.

But the good thing was that Dr. Frey told us all that the human spirit should have enjoyment. Excursions were coming up.

That's why Bella complained to me,

"How come we don't get to go to the Ostrich Farm?"

"Because it's the boys' turn.

"But we need enjoyment. He said that. Didn't you hear?"

"But we get to go to Eastlake Park. Didn't you hear that?"

Chapter 12

EASTLAKE PARK, AN ESCAPE

I loved Eastlake Park. We got to go boating in the lagoon and have lemonade and cookies at the pavilion. I couldn't understand why Bella wasn't happy to go there.

The day of our trip we stood at the gate, waited for the cars to pull up outside. Mrs. Mack ran back and forth like a spinning top. The boys gathered on the far side. They were not patient like us girls. They got out of line, pushed and whistled and leaned against the fence. We girls were supposed to act ladylike. Still and all, we did our share of shoving, but quieter.

Rachel-Ann re-tied the navy blue bow beneath the collar of my new blouse. I straightened the pleats on her skirt.

"Don't you wish Helen could go on this trip with us?" she said.

"I know. She asked me if I could go to the movies with her one Saturday. I had to tell her no."

"They're planning a trip for us to a movie theater next month."

"I know. We get to see Charlie Chaplin. Hey, Bella. Where are you going?"

She didn't answer, walked over to the boys. I saw her talking to some, then she stomped back. She passed me on the way to her friends who were fidgeting at the other end of the fence.

"Wait. Come back here. What were you saying to them?"

She reeled back. "It's okay, Celia. I wanted someone to bring me back an ostrich feather. I asked Julius first, but he didn't want to, thinks I'm a baby. But David said he would."

"The boys are real cranky these days," Rachel-Ann said.

"They are?"

"Of course you never noticed." Bella smiled at me. "It's their new housemother. They hate her."

"I knew that," Rachel-Ann said.

"I never saw her. What's she like?"

"They said she has a beard. And she hits them."

"Does Dr. Frey know that?'

Bella shrugged. She left me and Rachel-Ann and went off to go with some girls her own age.

"I'm glad we still have Mrs. Mack in our new cottage," I said. "And I'm glad Bella's not considered one of the babies any more. The little ones have to stay home. If I got to go on this outing and Bella didn't, she'd annoy me about it for days."

"It wouldn't be your fault."

Rachel-Ann was a good friend, always took my part.

"Look. Here comes a car." Rachel-Ann and the others stared through the openings in the wrought iron gate.

"I think that's Mr. Newmark's auto. He's here for the boys."

Mrs. Mack ushered them out. She reached out her hand, slicked back the hair on a messy one's head. Dr. Frey came out of his office and walked to the gate to help see the boys off.

While the girls were left waiting he talked to us in his loud, important-sounding voice, with his funny Austrian accent.

"Your turn next, young ladies. Manners are important. Always tell them thank you when they do something nice for you."

"We know." Bella mumbled. She kicked at the grass.

I bent down, whispered in her ear. "Shut up."

"And again, I want you should know who the volunteers are to give you this outing. Cars donated by..." He looked at his list. "Young Phil Newmark, Mr. Hoffman, Mr. Marshutz, Mrs. Meyer and Mr. Levy, all outstanding members of our board. They will attend our next celebration. They'll be judges in the recitation contest."

He couldn't speak longer because his words would be drowned out by the motor noises and screeches of brakes from the cars pulling up on the street outside our gate.

We piled into the cars. I managed to squeeze in beside Rachel-Ann on the back seat of a town car. Rachel-Ann said, "Are you going to try for a prize in the recitations?"

I nodded. "I'm memorizing a long poem. The Midnight Ride of Paul Revere. How about you?"

"I don't know. Help me think of something."

"Maybe we can find something from our school program that you can use at the Home, so you won't have to do two different ones."

"Would that be cheating?"

"No." I shut my eyes tight. "Maybe my mom will be well enough to come hear us."

"Will you invite her?"

"What do you think? You know I will. But she's probably not well yet. I don't want to talk about it."

We looked out the windows. The green treetops branched up and out between the telegraph wires. Maybe they were reaching for something like I was reaching for Mama in my mind.

At Eastlake Park I got to be in a rowboat with Rachel-Ann. The air felt warm. The water, when I stuck my hand down the side of the boat, felt warm, also. Dragon flies buzzed about. Strands of ferns and other plants lined the shore. We could feel their feathery leaves as we glided by, so close. Leaves dropping from the trees made ripples in the green and gray water. The faded white paint on our boat looked bad, but the wood had a sturdy feel under our feet.

Alice and some of the older girls got to row canoes. Those were always in danger of tipping, so I was glad our rowboat had a flat bottom.

Our oars barely passed through the water, we drifted and circled around. The sun felt just right when were in the open. Then when we drifted under the willow tree boughs the shade felt good too. My eyes closed. I didn't give a thought to school, to home with

Mama, to the Orphan's Home or anything. But Rachel-Ann had other thoughts.

"Leonard likes you," she said. "Do you like him back?"

"You mean like a boyfriend? No. Who told you he likes me?"

"Helen, of course. You know who she likes?"

"No."

"Julius. He grew tall this year. She thinks he's cute. And do you know who likes Leonard?"

"I don't even care."

"Ethel. Helen said so."

"Ethel? He doesn't pay any attention to her. Look. Over there. She's in that boat with the new girl."

A rowboat on the other side of the lagoon seemed intent on moving across the water toward us.

"It's Ethel. What does she think she's doing?"

Her boat moved steadily on. Then I noticed Bella in a canoe also coming along in our direction from under the Japanese Bridge. What in the world was she doing in a canoe? Oh, Alice was with her.

Bella waved her hand when she saw that Rachel-Ann and I were looking at her. Alice pushed Bella's arm down. If Bella stood up surely she'd knock them both in the water.

"Both those boats are headed our way, Celia. Row. Come on. Let's move away."

I pulled my oar faster. I wasn't so good at this. I tried to get us closer to the shore. Rachel-Ann's oar went in the wrong direction. Or was it mine? Either way, we seemed headed right for the other two boats. "Hey. It looks like we're all going to end up bumping into each other."

"Celia! It's shallow here. Push your oar in the ground. Help me push us away from those boats!"

"I'm trying." I looked up.

Ethel's boat slowed, almost stopped, came close to us. Ethel quit rowing, sat with her mouth open, looked like a fish waiting for bait. From the other side Alice maneuvered her canoe alongside us. Bella waved and shouted,

"Look at me. I got to ride in a canoe."

It looked to me like we were going to bump into them. But Ethel's boat drifted back. Alice's didn't. Rachel-Ann furiously pushed and rowed, splashing, the boat not making any progress. Bella stood half-way up.

She was going to tip her canoe. Alice called out, "Girls. Be careful. Don't do anything. Stay where you are."

But Bella wasn't paying attention. I felt our boat veer toward theirs on its own. It floated the opposite way we were pushing, right alongside where Bella acted so excited. Without thinking, I got up and reached across to stop Bella from standing. My boat tipped to the side. Just enough to make me lose my balance.

Splash! I landed on my side in wet, yucky, slimy water, which had looked so pretty from above, but looked dark and ugly now.

Rachel-Ann was right. Shallow water here. I could stand in the muck. The water came to my knees. I stood. I dripped. The water from my clothes and hair mixed with my tears, which I tried to hold back.

"I'll get the fellows from the boat house," Alice called out. "You all stay here. And, Bella, sit. Don't move a muscle." Alice pushed her canoe to the bank, steadied it so it was wedged in the reeds, nimbly jumped across to the bank. We watched her lift her skirts up and run down the path along the shore.

I couldn't stay in that cold water. I waded to the bank. My shoes sloshed. So hard to step up in the green mess of leaves and peels of bark. But I climbed on shore, shaking, headed for the boathouse, followed Alice. I heard the other girls in the boats behind me all talking at once. But I couldn't hear what they were saying.

I was afraid that the others would make fun of me when we got back. Bella tells me I'm too sensitive. But I'm not. I shook my head back and forth.

The fellow from the boathouse ran to me, wrapped me in a towel and got one of the chaperones to take me home to change. I didn't even get to take tea with the others in the pavilion.

No one said anything mean to me at supper that night. In the dorm in our new cottage the only girl who mentioned what happened was the new girl.

"I'm sorry about what happened at the lake," she said.

"Thanks. That's okay." I almost warned her to never be partners with Ethel. That could only be bad luck. But I held my tongue. She'd find out soon enough. Or maybe she wouldn't. Maybe Ethel was not as mean as she used to be.

After lights out Bella came to my bed and whispered to me, "Maybe they shouldn't've let me in the canoe. But I begged to ride in one. They wanted me to sit in a flat boat with some other girl, but I begged. So, nice old Alice said I could go with her."

"She's not old, but she is nice. Too nice. You go to sleep."

The Escape

When school started in September we were happy to be in our new cottage.

Bella stood beside me, looked at our images in the mirror, primped.

"This is great, Celia. We don't have to push each other away with these new mirrors."

"And we have more drawers in the dressers we share."

"And new sinks."

"We're not so crowded."

She giggled, "And new toilets."

"Uh huh." I smiled. She'd know soon enough why we older girls needed privacy in the toilets.

"But we still have to make our beds real good," she said.

"And keep everything spic and span."

Everyone around us was hurrying to get to ready for school. When we walked out into the bright sunshine in the yard we noticed a crowd of boys standing around the door to their cottage.

"I wonder what's going on over there?" Naturally it was Bella who said that out loud. But we all had to be wondering, too.

Rachel-Ann linked her arm in mine. "Let's not be late, Celia. Come on." She pulled me along, her curls bobbed up and down about her head.

Half way to the gate I turned around to look back at the boys. I saw Bella running away from where she'd been talking to her friend David. The housemother's back was to me so I couldn't see her face. But I saw the crowd of boys break apart, start off toward the gate, running behind me and Rachel-Ann and some other girls, as we headed out toward school.

Rachel-Ann and I walked pretty slow along the route to school. So it wasn't surprising that the fellows passed us.

At the corner the sidewalk led straight to the lawn by the school. But instead of taking this route four or five of them stopped. It didn't seem like they wanted to come inside.

I was about to ignore them and walk past, but Julius broke away from his friends, came up to me, said,

"You got any money? Can you give me a few cents?"

He held out his palm and showed me a little collection of pennies.

"What do you need it for?"

"The streetcar. I'm getting out of this place."

Rachel-Ann reached into her pocket, fished out a few cents. I had some in my pencil box but it was too hard to get to.

"Where're you going?" I asked.

"Home."

Now all the fellows came to stand around and listen.

"What about your brother?" I figured Abraham, his older brother, already at school, wasn't the kind to break the rules, to get up and leave like that.

"He can stay. She leaves him alone. He's too big to hit."

Rachel-Ann's eyes opened wide.

She looked down at his knickers, high top shoes. "You know the way?"

"Yeah."

"Who's home at your house?" I asked.

"I don't know. I think my dad moved. I got a big sister, Blossom. She's on her own. Maybe I can go there."

One of his friends patted him on the back. "Good luck. You can make it."

"Yeah, good luck."

The school bell sounded clear and loud.

"We better go."

Julius started toward the streetcar island, a concrete area in the middle of the street, under strings of trolley wires. He turned back and shouted to us, "Don't tell them at the Home, okay?"

The other boys, Rachel-Ann and me, we all nodded.

He held out his hand, palm up. "Swear it?"

The others held their palms up. So did I. They spit in their hands. That meant a promise. So I spit, too.

We ran off to our separate classrooms.

At recess I couldn't wait to tell Helen what happened. "I promised not to tell anyone at the Home, but I can tell you."

"I thought they were nice to you in that place."

"Not always." Then I told her about the housemother with a beard and a bad temper. After that I got involved in school stuff and didn't give it another thought.

Nobody missed Julius until dinner time. Then the questions started. The boys who were with him didn't say a word. Out on the grounds after dinner Dr. Frey gathered us all together.

"If any one of you have any idea where he can be you need to tell to us. We called to his father on the telephone and he has not seen him. He, you can imagine, is worried. We all are."

I trembled inside. I was one of the ones who knew he'd gone off on the streetcar. Bella didn't know. She probably would have told. Maybe not. But it was awful for me. I'd promised. I looked at Rachel-Ann. She shook her head. My hands shook. I licked my lips

How could I lie? It was killing me.

"We will have to call to the police. Go back to your cottages."

Rachel-Ann walked back with me, got me alone and whispered, "You almost told. We promised," she reminded me. "Don't forget."

At night in bed I felt tormented. Always good to be loyal. But to who? But then, what did I really know? Nothing. Where he went? No. I knew that he started off on a streetcar. That wasn't anything. But wasn't I supposed to tell what I knew?

The next day it was worse. Some kids told that they saw me and Rachel-Ann and David at the corner talking to Julius. So two policemen called us together after school to question us. They had black uniforms, big ugly guns in straps around their huge chests. And mustaches under heavy flat hats with brims trimmed in gold braid. They were so much taller than David and us. I was so scared I couldn't even talk. That's the main reason I didn't tell. Not out of loyalty to Julius. Just out of pure fear. Inside, my stomach churned. My heart raced. I couldn't even speak.

I've never been so frightened in my whole life. Not even when I woke up in the dark with nightmares. My mouth was dry. My feet froze in place. I knew I had to tell, but the others were as still as dummies. I couldn't turn my head to look at them. Or turn my head up to look at the policemen. There must have been ice, not blood in my veins. It would take a super effort to make any sound, let alone tell them that Julius might be at his sister's and that I saw him take a streetcar.

My mouth pried itself open. I let out air from holding my breath. I finally lifted my eyes. But what did I see? The police talking to each other and walking away. They went to the office with Dr. Frey. We were left alone. None of us moved at first. Then, slow as melting ice cream, the boys walked off to their cottage. Rachel-Ann didn't wait for me. She walked to ours without a word.

I managed to walk as soon as my arms and legs unfroze. I went to bed and had bad dreams.

I did have one good dream where I took the streetcar myself and Mama helped me climb up and sat with me. We smiled at each other. But that dream slipped away fast. The nightmares stayed.

At school I got Helen alone. "Will you do me a favor?"

"Sure. What?"Copy in your handwriting the note I'm going to write when we get back in class And don't tell Rachel-Ann."

"What's that all about?"

"You'll understand when you read it."

"Let's go play ball."

The note I had her copy said, "Ask the housemother about Julius. She knows why he left. Because of her. He went home to his big sister Blossom or to his father. Anonymous."

The next problem would be how to get the note to Dr. Frey. He wouldn't be able to trace the handwriting to me because it wasn't mine. I folded the paper up into a small square and kept it in my pocket on the way home.

I should have had Helen write the director's name on the message. I'd have to do it myself. I used crayon and disguised my writing by making funny squiggles around the letters. Bella came over and wanted to see what I was doing. I told her it was an art project for school so she went away. I was able to deposit the message in the ingoing mailbox on the front counter when nobody was looking.

Two days later Julius was back. He wouldn't talk about what happened. When any of us kids asked him he just said he had a good time, but not where or what. But the main thing was this–the day he came back there was a new housemother in the boys' cottage. Nobody talked about her, either. Except they said she wasn't particularly nicer than the old one. But she left them mostly alone, sat in a chair and read magazines all day.

Chapter 13

School, High Holy Days, October

I liked the new semester because I had a lot more friends besides Helen. Plus I liked my new teacher, so nice. But what I liked best, we were going to study what she called literature. Literature means stories, and how I loved stories.

I wasn't happy when the Jewish High Holy Days came later in September, because I could not join my class for two days. Rosh Hashanah came first, then at the end of the week Yom Kippur, another day to stay out to say prayers and learn the rituals, so I'd miss our literature lessons at school.

I asked Helen to show me her assignment sheet when I came back after Rosh Hashanah.

At lunchtime we walked out of our class together onto the playground.

"Why couldn't you come to school? What's that holiday for?" Helen asked.

"Because it's the beginning of the world. It's the end of the Harvest. Because we celebrate the beginning of our New Year. We're supposed to think back, like if you did anything wrong you've got to ask for forgiveness."

"Sounds like confession to me. Did you do anything wrong, Celia?"

"Lots of things. I always ask for forgiveness. Not just on this day." I skipped a few steps.

We reached the outdoor lunch tables that had benches attached and sat down together.

"So what do you do when you stay home from school?

"Mostly the boys sit in the synagogue and say special prayers. Oh, one good part. We get to eat apples dipped in honey."

"Yum," Helen said, motioning Rachel-Ann to come sit with us. We made room.

Rachel-Ann opened her lunch bag. "Tell about the shofar, Celia. Tell her."

"Oh, the shofar's just a horn. A ram's horn."

Rachel-Ann said, "The horn's long and crooked. And it makes a sound when they blow into it."

"Nuhh uh. It doesn't sound like a real horn,"

Rachel-Ann frowned at me. "Oh yes It does. That thing makes a screechy noise."

"Does it come from a real ram?" Helen wanted to know.

"Yes, but it's ancient. That's what they did in ancient times. They didn't have trumpets like we have." I wished Rachel-Ann wouldn't keep talking to Helen about our shofar.

"The angels blew horns." Helen took a bite of her sandwich. "At least in pictures. And they played harps."

"Yeah, I've seen those pictures, and they blew real long horns and trumpets while they flew around, didn't they?"

Helen nodded.

More kids came to sit at our table now. I didn't feel like talking about our holidays any more. Too many questions would come up. And half the time I wouldn't know what to answer. I listened to the others chat and took a bite of my crispy red apple.

I had a secret hope that I didn't even share with Bella. I thought I heard Mrs. Mack tell Alice that the parents of the half orphans could come to our holy day services in our synagogue on the last day. Maybe Mama would be well enough to attend.

The day before Yom Kippur we had an early dinner with lots

of good food—challah, sweet bread, honey to symbolize a sweet new year ahead, sweetened cooked carrots, dates and little chunks of tender meat. We ate fast so we could finish before the sun went down. That's when the fasting began. Those who fasted had to wait till the sun went down the next day before they could eat anything.

But Dr. Frey said children under thirteen did not have to fast. I just made it. I was twelve and a half now. Poor Abraham and Leonard already had their thirteenth birthdays. They'd had a ceremony in the synagogue where Dr. Frey proclaimed them to be bar mitzvah boys.

That day I had sat in the temple and watched them say the Hebrew prayers they'd learned. They also had to tell Dr. Frey in English that they'd now take part in grown-up things, now they could call themselves men. Ha! My friends and I couldn't stop giggling. They were still boys. Especially compared to the Rabbi and Dr. Frey. Leonard's white prayer shawl slipped off his shoulder, so the fringes dragged along the floor. I guess it didn't bother him because his speech sounded pretty good.

Both those boys had grown fast since they'd become bar mitzvahs. But they still looked like kids next to all those grown-ups.

On Yom Kippur we sat in the temple all morning and followed along in our little prayer books while the rabbi chanted. In the afternoon session there came a pause. The rabbi left the shofar on the podium. Bella whispered that she wanted to try blowing it.

"You better not," I said.

Later, when we were excused and the kids were milling about, Bella saw her chance. She snuck up to the table in front of the Torah. The Torah is the sacred book I used to stare at during the service except when the rabbi took it out and kissed it. It looked like a huge decorated scroll wound around two wooden handles that rested in a case called an ark that was lined with blue velvet. The table in front had a blue velvet covering, too. That's where they'd set the horn down.

Bella looked behind her to see if I was watching. Lots of people walked around so even I didn't notice her until she caught my eye. Oh, no. She wouldn't. She did. Bella picked up the shofar and put it to her mouth. I could see her cheeks fill with air. No sound came out.

I froze in my tracks. What trouble she would get into! I hoped the rabbi and Dr. Frey were too busy to look at her!

The boys saw her. Especially the little ones. They came up and grabbed the shofar out from Bella's hand. Three of them took turns trying to blow it. A few creaky sounds came out. I saw the rabbi look up. Still talking to Dr. Frey while he walked, he went up to the front of the temple, took the shofar from the littlest boy's hands, kept talking to Dr. Frey without saying a word to the boy, put the shofar up high on another shelf and shoed away the boys . They went back to their seats.

Bella grinned at me. No one had noticed her. "I see you weren't able to make any sound with it, my dear," I said.

"That's because you have to practice a lot, my dear. Maybe I'll be a rabbi when I grow up and then I'll learn to blow it and make a nice loud sound, my dear."

"Ha. Maybe you'll be a Mrs. Rabbi. And your husband won't let you touch that horn, either."

I heard her mutter as she sat down with her legs crossed, "I can be whatever I want to be."

What just happened must have given the rabbi a new idea for his next sermon to us. He read to us, "The shofar is blown in long, short and staccato blasts that follow a set sequence."

Rabbi Tabachnick picked up the shofar to demonstrate. I wanted to cover my ears when he blew the long ones. Such screeches. But the short sounds sounded like a more like a soft cry, maybe for peace. The rabbi left the table.

Mrs. Mack came running up the aisle, whispered to Dr. Frey. 'Yes, yes," I heard him say.

Dr. Frey called out, "The symbolic reason for the sounds. Who remembers?"

Leonard raised his hand. "It reminds us of when we got the Ten Commandments, it reminds us of Abraham's sacrifice of his son, it reminds us to repent to atone for our misdeeds, and more like that."

Dr. Frey sighed. "Yes, Leonard, and more like that. We will together go over it more in Hebrew class."

By this time I could see that none of the parents had come to join us. Good thing I'd never told Bella my hope that Mama would come. One day she will. We would have to wait.

The rabbi had been out of the room during the break. He rushed back now, his black coattails flew behind him like crows. He faced us, and we all sat down. He told us to follow him in reciting the appropriate prayers.

Later, outside, I whispered to Leonard, "Do you really understand all that Hebrew the rabbi says?"

"Yes. You can study Hebrew, too.

"I already know how to write Yiddish. My Mother taught me."

But you can learn Hebrew, too. Girls are allowed nowadays. We live in modern times now, the nineteen hundreds."

"I know. Women can sit with the men in some modern synagogues now."

"Do you think that's a good idea?"

"Yes. It's reformed." I turned and walked away.

We saw another month begin when we returned to school. September was over, then came October, the month with Halloween, Helen didn't say anything about another party at her house this year.

It was a few days before the thirty-first when I finally asked her.

"Don't you think I would have invited you by now if we planned a party?"

"I wasn't sure."

"Well, we're not. My mom's tired of all the fuss. My brothers are older now and don't care about Halloween parties. We're going trick or treating. Wanna come with us?"

"I'll ask permission."

"Get a costume. I'm going to be a gypsy."

"I could do that, too."

"I bet Leonard won't want to wear his same costume this year."

"Why not?"

"Don't you remember? Maybe you didn't see it. Last year they sewed patches on his clothes, and they were old clothes to begin with. He was supposed to be a tramp. One of the guys went up to him and said,

"What are you supposed to be, an orphan?"

"Oh. What did he answer?"

"He walked away. I think he was crying, went in the back yard under a tree in the dark."

"That was so mean."

"I know. 'Cause that mean boy laughed at him, too."

"Oh." I opened my book.

I felt real bad. If that guy thought it was bad to be an orphan, and Bella and I, we lived in an orphanage, so what did Helen think? If Helen felt sorry for me, I wouldn't want to be friends with her. I wouldn't even ask at the Home if I could go trick or treating with her. They probably wouldn't let me anyway. But now I would not even want to.

Other things were happening at the Home these days. I didn't need to be with school friends to have a nice time.

First the directors took us to a movie theater. It was Hamburger's Theater on Broadway and Eighth downtown. We got to see Mary Pickford.

"Do you think those little kids in the front row can read the words?" Rachel-Ann whispered.

"Yeah, but if not, they could guess. You see the actors move their lips, and they make themselves look so sad, so happy, so mad, you can tell."

The music got slow. A lady in a skinny dress got a broom and hit at the girl till she fell on the floor. Rachel-Ann sobbed. "They're treating that girl so bad."

The man behind me tapped my shoulder and told me to be quiet so I had to wait to the end when we all filed out to tell her what I thought.

"Mary was supposed to be an orphan girl, but she was a grown up lady. And that lady who hit her wasn't even in the orphanage. She was just a mean person. I didn't like that part."

"Well, I loved the whole thing."

In November they told us that a restaurant invited all fifty-nine of us, including the babies, for Thanksgiving dinner. I got pretty excited and so did Bella. We checked the calendar, hoped it would come soon. I only wished the parents could be there, but they weren't invited. Anyway, Mama was still sick.

Helen stopped by my desk. "Are you mad at me?" she asked. You're not eating lunch with me these days."

"No, I'm not mad."

"Is it because I didn't have a Halloween party?"

"Of course not."

The bell rang. We walked out of the classroom together. "Helen, it's not that. You know? You know, what I mean is, you know I'm only a half orphan. I'm not a whole orphan."

"Yes, I know. But, Celia, I'd like you if you were half or whole or anything. I don't care about that."

"And…" I started to cry. "And Rachel-Ann and Julius, they have fathers. And I …"

I couldn't finish. I burst into loud sobs.

Rachel-Ann put her arm around me. She walked me around the corner of the building where no one could see us. I put my head in my hands, cried and cried.

"That's okay, Celia. It doesn't matter."

"It's not th…th…at." My sobs made my whole body shake. "My Papa's dead, but I'm not even sure if I'm still a half orphan. My mom never answered my last letter. I haven't heard from her in a very long t….t….t...time."

Helen patted me on the back. "It's okay. You would have heard."

I took out my crochet-edged hankie and wiped my eyes.

"Let's sit down. Here's a bench." Twigs and leaves littered the bench because almost no one sat here under this tree behind the bungalow. Helen brushed off the seat.

We tucked our skirts under us, sat.

"So when was the last time you wrote to her?"

I thought back. "It was quite a while ago."

"Can't you ask your housemother about your mother?"

"I'm afraid of what she'll say. And I do NOT want Bella to hear me, either."

"You have to be patient."

"That's all I can do. We need to go back now." A few dry leaves blew down from the tree behind us, fell on the asphalt in front of us, skittered away as I stepped over them.

School kept me busy, plus my chores at the home. More folding in the laundry, weeding the garden, and I had to help with the chicken coop now, too. Being friends with Helen again felt terrific. I didn't spend any time thinking about my fears for Mama. Until the day the teacher spoke to us about our end-of-the-year program.

Our class had to present a performance. The teacher chose Helen to give a speech. I had to recite a poem.

A few days earlier Rachel-Ann had told me, all excited, that they picked her to sing a solo at the end-of-the-year program in her class. "The whole class has to learn a new song, but I get to sing alone. I'm so happy. But I'm scared, too."

"You'll do great. Besides, look how much time you have to practice. The end of the term is months away."

"Yeah, I know. And the teacher told us to invite our parents to come and watch our show."

That spoiled it for me.

Helen glanced at me. I kept my head down, eyes on my desk. I didn't want her to see how that made me feel. I guess she understood, even though I tried to act cheerful. She never mentioned the program to me after that.

When we finished supper we were supposed to go right back to the cottages to do our homework. I stopped to go talk to Mrs. Mack.

"Do you think my mother will be well by June?"

"I did hear she's getting much better."

"Really? Then maybe she can come to our presentation. We're supposed to invite our parents."

"Yes, they do every year. Remember last year?"

"Well, Mama was very sick then."

"Listen, Celia. If the parents can't come, we send a representative from the Home. One of the ladies from the Jewish Benevolent Society or someone we know. That works out fine. After all, not all the parents of the other children from that school can come, either. Many have to work. And June is a long time from now. Not to worry."

"It's just that… If my mom is well enough… Did you really hear that she's better?"

"Yes. As a matter of fact, Dr. Frey told me she's a lot better now."

The air in the room seemed lighter. I hummed a little song on my way out—one that Mama and Papa had taught us.

Bella caught up with me in the cottage when we were getting ready for bed.

"Guess what?"

"Well, let me brush my teeth. What?" I spit toothpaste into the sink.

"My class is having an end-of-the-year program and I get to say a poem."

"Well, guess what? My class is, too. And Mrs. Mack says Mama may be well enough to come and be in the audience."

"Really?" Bella did a little dance right there by the sink.

"But if she needs more time to recover, one of those ladies might come. But I hope they don't send the one who wore the fur coat when we got measured. She's too fancy."

"Oh, I wish Mama had a fur coat."

"I don't, Bella. Mama would look out of place here."

Chapter 14

Thanksgiving at A. L. Levy's Restaurant

The next thing to occupy us was the Thanksgiving dinner. Again we had to dress up in our best clothes.

"Bella, would you like me to tie your bow?"

"No, Celia. I can do it. See you later."

I watched my little sister walk to the end of her row of beds. Two of her friends waited for her at the cottage door, linked arms with hers, and walked out the door, skipping together.

Since Bella turned nine she didn't take the time to show me letters she wrote, or her schoolwork. She never told me the things she and her friends talked about anymore, either.

I went back to brushing my hair, still thin and wispy, but a lot longer now. I made two braids, puffed them around in circles by my ears. Rachel-Ann came up and stood in front of me so other girls wouldn't see. She reached in her pocket and pulled out a small round box, lifted the lid. We both looked down at some orangey-red stuff.

"Put a little of this on your lips, Celia, and then a bit more on your cheeks. We want to look nice tonight."

"Is that rouge? I don't think we should."

"Use your pinkie. Just get a little on and be delicate when you put it on. Don't rub hard."

I nodded, took a deep breath. "Okay. I'll try."

My pinkie felt cold when it touched the rouge, but kind of nice, too. I smoothed some on my lips. Rachel-Ann nodded. I dipped my pinkie in again and applied it to the top of my cheeks. Then I ran to a mirror, peaked in, and screamed loud.

"Look at me, I look horrible. This isn't pretty, Rachel-Ann. I look like a circus person." I got a hankie out of my pocket, rubbed hard, took all the rouge off. Still a slight pink glow stayed on my skin. My face looked much nicer than when the whole area was covered.

"You're right. You look much better, Celia. See mine? Mine's real faint, too. Are you ready?"

We joined the rest of the children who lined up outside by the gate. A group of limousines sent by the Workman and Newmark families stood ready along the street. Mrs. Mack and Dr. Frey read off their lists.

A driver in an olive green uniform opened the door of a long black car. Some smaller girls in frilly dresses climbed into the middle seat. I wore a navy blue dress, trimmed in what Mrs. Mack said was ecru-colored lace. She said it was elegant.

Rachel-Ann and I slid into the farthest back seat by ourselves. She leaned in close to me and whispered, "Let's sit with the boys at the restaurant. You know that Leonard likes you. I bet we can sit with him and David and those guys."

"You keep telling me that. I don't care. I'm not boy crazy."

"Humph. Neither am I. Celia, don't think that about me. I get so tired of being with girls all the time. Let's mix up."

Our cars stopped downtown on Spring Street, near Sixth. It was a busy part of town, with tall buildings and lots of traffic, clothing stores and streetcars. My heart beat fast when I looked out the window. I'd been on this street before. In fact, lots of times. Mama took me shopping here. There was that funny shop with polka dot dresses in the window, the barbershop with the pink striped pole in front, the stationery store that sold fountain pens. Too expensive she said, I remember.

The driver got out, straightened his cap, opened the limousine door, watched the kids pile out. He escorted the smaller ones to the huge doors made of beautiful wood at the entrance. I pulled Rachel-Ann aside before we got there, led her to the corner.

"Look down there." I pointed to the streetcar tracks running along the road into the distance where you couldn't see any farther.

"Where?"

"There". Sunshine still came down through the treetops along the street and lit up the road, not yet supper time, still light out. But it was too far to see the end of the road. My breaths came fast. "That's how you get to my house."

"You mean where you used to live?"

"Yes." I rushed my words together. "I bet I can get on the next streetcar and go all the way home."

"But your mom's not there."

"No, but my big brother Sam lives there. My uncle got a housekeeper to stay there nights before he went back to New York. She can stay until Mama gets well."

I stood on one foot then the other. I felt all shaky to see how close we were. But Rachel-Ann pointed to the kids from the other cars who poked each other, laughed and crowded around the entrance. Mrs. Mack turned in our direction, away from helping them inside, waved to get us over there. Rachel-Ann took my arm and walked me to them. I calmed myself down, walked at her pace.

Inside the restaurant, through the dim light, I saw two extra-long tables covered with sparkling white linen cloths and rows and rows of shiny forks and spoons that looked like real silver. A chandelier made of what looked like thousands of crystals hung from the ceiling, sending rainbows of light on the walls, even on us. At the end of the large room gold-framed paintings of important looking men stood out against walls made of the same dark wood as the doors.

Alice took charge of the little ones, placed them in seats near the far wall. Most of the boys sat at the long table near the entrance. That's where Rachel-Ann led me, pushed me down in the chair nearest the entrance. Then she sat herself down between me and Leonard.

She poked his shoulder, said, "Guess what, Leonard."

"What?" He looked at his silverware, picked up his spoon, stared at his reflection in the silver, set it back down. A strand of his blond wavy hair fell over his forehead. "What?"

"Celia lives down the block from here."

"That's not what I said!" I had to lean forward so I could see Leonard past Rachel-Ann's head full of bouncing curls.

"But close. Isn't it close, Celia?"

"Not really. Well, pretty far, but straight down the line. Down Spring Street where it curves onto Central for a while, and on then to my street."

"Could you walk there? Tonight?"

"No. I couldn't." Of course not. But the idea of sneaking out of the restaurant and heading down that way gave me an odd thrill. I felt a tightening in my chest. I sat still in my chair, hoped no one could tell.

"Here comes the food." Leonard picked up his fork. The rest of us unfolded our napkins like they'd told us to do so we could spread them on our laps and cover our good clothes.

The boys did it so showy, flipped them out, waved them like flags, each put a corner under his belt.

Waiters came around carrying platters and platters of great-smelling roast turkey, mashed potatoes and stuffing, to heap steaming hot on our plates.

"Pretty fancy," Rachel-Ann said. She bent her head over her plate and said, "Smells delicious."

I scanned the tables, searching for Bella. She sat with some girls her age at the table across from ours. I stared at her bobbed hair until I got her attention. She looked back at me, grinned.

I waved my fork at her, smiled back, pointed at the plate. She nodded, rubbed her tummy, a sign she thought the food would be great. Some of the kids were already stuffing their mouths full of food.

Oh, no. The waiters stopped, stood still with their platters half full. Dr. Frey had signaled them. His thick hair waved over his forehead as he rushed past the tables to the far end. He wore a heavy-looking suit with a full, silk bow tie. His mustache turned up at the corners then came down low over his upper lips, but it did not get in the way of his mouth when he started a speech to all of us.

"Children. This is a day of giving thanks," he told us. He went on about the pilgrims and wanting freedom. Good words for us Jewish people who wanted to come to a country that did not discriminate against them. He kept on," So many of you children come from backgrounds of personal hardships." He said that was why we were orphans or half orphans, or foundlings, and why we needed and received aid and blessings, and we should all be so grateful on "this lovely day of Thanksgiving."

"When do we eat?" David said, leaning forward from his chair on the other side of Leonard, his lips open in a wide grin.

Was I glad it wasn't Bella who said that! It would be just like her. Then the waiters went on to serve everyone food. Waitresses came and filled our glasses with water that had ice in it. I loved that kind of water.

Leonard's mouth was so full that he sounded funny when he told David that I lived close, which wasn't what I'd said at all

I had to tell him, "I meant that I know the way because I took that streetcar there with my mom. Lots of times."

David's head popped up. "Maybe you could take the streetcar home tonight like Julius did before."

Rachel-Ann and Leonard laughed.

"No, I mean it." David dipped his piece of turkey into the gravy on his plate.

Rachel-Ann looked down the row, past Leonard, past David, past Morris and the other boys.

"Where's Abraham?" she asked Leonard.

"Didn't you know? Him and his brother went to live with some relative in Kentucky."

"Kentucky! How come we never knew?"

"Leonard shrugged. "We had a farewell party for them. After dinner. In our cottage. The housemother baked a chocolate cake with white frosting."

"Nobody invited us."

"It was just boys got invited. His father came at night to pick them up. We helped them pack their stuff. Julius had a lot more clothes than Abraham."

I chimed in. "Sure. The younger ones get our hand-me-downs."

David leaned across to talk to me and Rachel-Ann. "Their uncle don't got boys. He only got daughters. That's why he took them two guys. That's what Julius told me"

"Is that where Julius went that time he ran away?"

"Naw. Kentucky's too far, back east somewhere. He went with his big sis. Blossom. She's on her own. Too bad. His uncle got more money. He's a maker of false teeth."

"You mean a dentist?" I said.

"No. Julius bragged what a good artist he was back in the old country. So he knew how to be a sculptor. You know? A person who makes statues? Here he had to make false teeth."

That was so funny. Rachel-Ann and I and even Leonard laughed out loud.

David said, "Celia, you got enough money for streetcar fare?"

"Maybe, why?"

"You wanna go to your house?"

I gasped. "More than anything."

"Go tonight. Sneak away when the rest of us get into all those cars out there."

Leonard looked me in the eye. "Do you want to? I got money. I could even go with you."

I found my mouth opening and closing. I couldn't speak out any words. The thought of actually leaving this restaurant and escaping down Spring Street gave me the shivers.

"We can shelter you so they don't see you get away." Rachel-Ann's face beamed.

Good thing I couldn't bring myself to talk because my voice would have been drowned out anyway by the clatter of dishes and silverware. The waiters came to clear away our plates.

I still couldn't say anything, but Rachel-Ann said, "Look at that. We won't have to do kitchen duty like back at the Home." Leonard said Yeah under his breath.

Out from the back of the restaurant strode a cheerful looking, bald-headed man in a nice dark suit with thin lines up and down. He all but pushed Dr. Frey out of the way so he could talk to us from the same place at the back wall.

It was Mr. A. L. Levy himself, the man who had come to Los Angeles from Scotland to start this restaurant. Dr. Frey introduced him and told us he owned some taverns and other businesses, and lots of charities, too.

I calmed down just looking at him. I liked Mr. Levy. He looked so nice. He smiled right at us. He had a twinkle in his eye and a smile on his face, so that made it easy to believe him when he told us how welcome we were to eat in what he called his "establishment." "And now," he shouted with a trill, "Enjoy the dessert!"

A slice of pumpkin pie and a scoop of vanilla ice cream. For us. In crystal dishes. The waiters and waitresses ran back and forth, passed each other, balanced trays, passed out the desserts. Spoons clinked as we savored the cool delicacies. I glanced at David. He picked up his empty dish in both hands. On the dish's way toward his mouth Leonard slapped at his hand.

"Don't do that. You can't lick your plate."

Rachel-Ann shook her head. "You should know better."

The melted white cream and brown crumbs clinging to the bottom of the crystal looked tempting. It must have killed the boys not to lick up all the crumbs.

I guessed the kids forgot about me going home. What an exciting idea. But not real. I put my napkin on the table. But no, they didn't forget.

Rachel-Ann said, "How about it, Celia? Do you want us to stand front of you so you can get away to the streetcar stop?"

Leonard sat forward, past Rachel-Ann, looked me in the eye, and said, "David and her can walk with us to the corner. Then you and I can turn around the block and she and him will go back and no one will see that we're not with you guys. David, do you think that will work?"

We heard the noise of chairs moving, looked up to see that the dinner had ended. Most of the boys and girls stood up now. We pushed ourselves out of our chairs. Some of the others walked by us where we stood huddled off to one side. I watched Mrs. Mack and Alice hold the hands of the little ones on their way to the door to go outside. We four talked in whispers.

"I don't know..." I started.

"Are you afraid?"

I don't know why I didn't say yes. I felt almost as scared as I'd been the time the police came to ask me questions about Julius. My fast heartbeats started up again. My hands felt clammy. I held tight to the edge of the table.

"Look how happy she is," Rachel-Ann said. "I wish I lived close enough that I could get on a streetcar and go home to see my dad." Her voice trailed off. "But he'd be at work, anyway."

The restaurant people walked behind us, led us to the exit, sort of crowded us out the door. We were the last out onto the street. The buildings looked shadowy now that night had come and the streetlights lit their fronts and the sidewalks. David and Leonard walked fast past the crowd waiting for the limousines. Rachel-Ann took my arm and made me follow the boys.

What if Sam wasn't home? What if Dr. Frey or Mrs. Mack caught us? What if they called my mama at the sanitarium to tell on me? I was scared of all that. But I was more scared that my friends would think I was a coward. Maybe they'd think I didn't even want to leave our cottages at the Home.

Rachel-Ann said in a low voice, "That's really nice of Leonard. He doesn't want you to go alone, he must like you a lot."

"Uh, yeah." My mouth was dry.

We reached the corner. The clang of streetcars going in opposite directions added to the motor noises of cars. The dark sky made us look like shadows from a distance, but enough light came from the farther off streetlights to let us see the storefronts and people out walking.

Leonard held my elbow. "Wait till that truck goes by. Then we can turn. Sure you got enough coins?"

"Y...yes. In my pocket." I clutched at my skirt.

"Celia! Celia!"

We all turned to see Bella running toward us. She'd broken from the group of her friends when she spotted me, ran fast to our corner.

"Where you going? Celia, what're you doing?"

"Quiet." David got between her and me. "Don't let them see you. She's going home. Isn't that the way you live?" He pointed down Spring Street.

"Take me! Celia, Take me with you!"

"Do you have any money?" David asked her.

"No, I didn't bring any."

"Then you can't come with her." David turned his back.

"Wait." Leonard stopped in front of her. "I got money. You want to come with us?" He pushed his hand down into the pocket on his pant leg. Then a noise made him look up.

Too late.

Some of the nine-year-old girls in the crowd had followed Bella. Their voices and the honking cars blended into enough noise to cause the grownups to notice us on the corner where we stood. Mrs. Mack sent one of the chauffeurs to get us all back.

Leonard handed me the coins he'd taken from his pockets. "Maybe you can do this on your own." He broke away from our group, sauntered along the outer curb to the parked cars, didn't look back at me.

I trembled. Alone I could not do this.

I followed the others. We couldn't see in the windows of the storefronts because the streetlights didn't shine on them, everywhere looked dark now.

The chauffeurs stood stiff, held the car doors open wide, looked over our heads as we piled in.

We drove back the way we'd come. But the way seemed long and I didn't feel like joining in the chatter from the front seats.

No one from the Home ever found out what Leonard and I almost did.

That night Bella walked over to my bed, kneeled down so her head touched mine.

"Oh, Celia. I'm so sorry. If I knew you had a chance to go home and see Sammy I would never have spoiled it for you."

I smiled to myself. I felt safe here under the covers. Sneaking away and going off in the dark could have been dangerous. Who knew what dangers Bella saved me from.

"That's okay. When Mama gets well we'll both get to go home." I sat up, held out my arms. "Come here, baby."

She let me hug her. I hugged her shoulders, her back, and stroked her hair. "It shouldn't be so long now. Not long before we get to live in our house again, sleep in our old beds, eat at the table with Sam and Mama. Maybe, maybe pretty soon."

Chapter 15

Christmas, Chanukah, Passover, Mama, Leaving

Everyone loved our trip to A. L. Levy's restaurant. We had to write thank you notes afterwards. I wanted my note to be different because it looked like we all were going to write exactly the same thing.

I put my pencil in my mouth while I tried to think of what to say. I sat in the Home's little library, looked up at the ceiling.

I felt a bump. Oh, oh. Here came Ethel. She'd been leaving me alone since she'd made friends with the new girl, Eloise.

"What do you want?"

"Can I see your note?"

"Why?"

"I never know what to say."

"Write what the others are writing. Just say, 'Thank you for a very nice time. The food was delicious.' Or something like that."

"Is that what you're writing?"

"I guess so." I sighed. No point in trying to be original. It's just that my teacher at school always liked what I wrote. Sometimes she wrote in red pencil, 'very original.' Once I showed Bella my paper and she said, "You can write so good because you always read all those fairy tales and that gave you a good imagination." I kissed her for remembering that. She pushed me away, frowning, and walked away.

"Ethel, you're making me nervous."

I wrote out the words I'd said to her real fast. She sat down, took my paper, copied it in her own crooked handwriting, tossed mine back to me.

After Ethel left I added that the room was pretty and the servers nice, but that still wasn't original. Maybe they wouldn't even read all the notes, so I guess it didn't matter that I was not original this time.

The week before vacation the teacher decorated our classroom for Christmas. She hung up pictures of snowmen, Christmas trees, pine cones, jingle bells on horse-drawn carriages, and wreaths made from red and green construction paper. I thought our room looked beautiful.

For art lessons we got to use colored pencils instead of those fat crayons we used in earlier grades.

I folded a large paper in fourths. On the inside I drew a beautiful pine tree with colored balls on the branches, and presents underneath. On the outside square I wrote in fancy colors, Merry Christmas. Helen looked over at my art from her seat next to mine.

"That's so pretty. Is it going to be a card for your Mama at her place?"

"No, Helen. We don't celebrate Christmas."

"Oh, yes. Isn't that why you don't sing all the words when we sing Christmas carols?"

"Umm humm." I outlined a silver star on the top of my tree. "I told you I love the songs, and I know all the words, but it doesn't feel comfortable to say the parts about your religion."

"I remember. So who are you making the card for?"

"You'll see."

I folded a bigger piece of paper into an envelope. While Helen was busy coloring her own picture I wrote her name on the envelope. Inside, I wrote "From Your Friend Celia." When the bell rang I handed it to her.

"For me? Oh, Celia. I thought you were making it for the teacher."

"Nope. I want you to have it. You're my good friend."

"Thank you, Celia." She placed it with care inside her notebook.

The next day at school Helen handed me a store-bought Christmas card. The cover showed happy people in furs, riding in old fashioned carriages. I stared down at my desk, couldn't get out the words to thank her.

"Don't you like it?"

"Yes, but it makes me feel bad that I only got you a handmade one."

She reached out her hand to me. "Yours is more precious."

I shook my head no, relieved when the teacher chose that moment to tell us to open our arithmetic books. How could I explain that I felt stuck here in the Home and never had the chance to buy anything like a card.

On our way home from school one day I stopped Bella on the sidewalk, made her wait while I bent to re-tie her shoelaces. At dinner I watched her table manners. "Spoon your soup from the back." Then, when we took our dishes to the kitchen, I told her, "Stack yours so the forks don't fall off."

"Celia," she hissed at me. "Leave me alone."

Outside on the path to our cottage she grabbed hold of my arm. "What're you doing, Celia? Why do you keep bothering me all the time these days?" She dropped my arm and tried to walk in front of me. I grabbed her by the waist and held her back on the path.

"Listen, Bella. I don't think I'm bothering you. I'm just thinking what our mother would do if she was here."

"Well, you're not my mother. So quit telling me what to do all the time."

"Okay." I let her go on ahead. She had no idea what I was thinking. It had been a long time since we heard from Mama. I wondered what would happen if she never got well. I'd have to take care of Bella, and I thought I'd start now.

That weekend I followed Alice into her office, watched her roll paper into the carriage of her typewriter.

"Do you think you'll be a secretary?"

"I hope so. That's a good job for a lady."

"What was it like to be here, knowing no one was out there waiting for you? I mean…" I blushed. "I mean, well, you told me... It's just that…"

"Celia. Lately you've been following me around a lot. What's got into you?"

"Nothing. I'm sorry. I better go do my homework." I looked behind me, walked away, saw her put her eyes back on her typing paper.

At night I waited until everyone seemed to be asleep. I let myself think awful thoughts. I cried, hugged my pillow, my mouth muffled, my eyes watering into the cotton pillowcase.

I thought of Ethel. She would also be in the orphanage forever. But it made her nasty. I would never get like that. I would be kind, like Alice. I cried harder.

Chanukah came during school Vacation. I loved seeing the lighting of the candles. I even sat still, listened and nodded when Dr. Frey gave us his sermon on Obligation. He said the consciousness of responsibility and obligation lead morals into the right path. Yes, we'd be good.

Getting gold coins from our synagogue congregation became another happy event. And then we got a surprise when the Elk's Club of Huntington Park brought us all toys—baseballs, dolls, books, candy. So pleasant, I almost got over my worries. Then something happened to set me off again.

We got four new children. And they were only toddlers. Sisters and brothers. A boy two years old, a girl three, another boy five, and a girl six.

Mrs. Mack and Dr. Frey only told us that their parents had died. I tried to find out how but no one would tell me. Maybe they didn't know. They kept these kids upstairs, and Dr. Frey hired a nurse to help out with the toddler. The oldest girl came to our cottage.

"Mrs. Mack, can I help take care of them? I love babies."

"I think you worry about them losing their parents. Yes, you can help."

She gave me little tasks, like wiping the bibs on the smallest one, reading to the others, showing them how to sit at our breakfast table.

When I spooned oatmeal into the little boy's mouth he held out his hand to me, laughed. I laughed too, wiped his mouth, watched him reach his fist into his hair. Told him, "No, no." He put down his hand, opened his mouth for more.

They were all four well behaved, not bratty like some little kids act.

On our last day of vacation I went looking for Mrs. Mack, found her in the library.

"Mrs. Mack," I said to her "Will these kids always stay here?"

"Probably not, Celia. We like to find adoptive parents for our whole orphans. But it's hard when we try to keep siblings together. Four is a big number to handle."

"Oh, Mrs. Mack. Do keep them together. If I had to be separate from Bella when I came here, I don't know what I'd have done."

"Don't worry about it. Dr. Frey has some ideas."

She set some books on a shelf. "Let's sit down, Celia. I have some good news for you. I was going to wait to tell you until I was certain. But I almost am. "

I sat still, leaned in to her, waited.

"Your mother tested clear. Her coughing is near normal. She can come visit again."

"Really? When?" I tilted my head to the side, bit my lip, waited.

"Soon. She has to be tested all the time, you know. Her sputum, that's her spit, yes, you know that, it had to be clear for a certain length of time before they are sure she's completely cured. But in the meantime she can come visit. Last time they let her it was too soon. Her coughing came back after that."

"Yeah, I guess that's why she never came back after last time. What about her… You know…"

"No, I don't know, Celia. What?" She rearranged some pencils on the desk at her side."

"You know, her melancholy. Her sad, depressed feelings." I lowered my head. "You told me before that it was hard for her to get over Papa and Abraham…you know."

"Better. All around better. You'll see yourself."

I got up, walked to the door, turned back, looked at her and said, "Shall I tell Bella? Or wait till you say when?"

"Tell, tell. She should be happy, too."

But I wouldn't let myself feel happy. What if something happened before she could come? What if?

The sun streamed in through the high-up windows in our cottage on the day of Mama's visit. March usually dawned cold in Huntington Park, but today would probably turn hot.

Bella primped in front of our mirror. She wore her best dress with the dropped waist, red plaid pleats below it.

"Aren't you going to comb your hair, Celia?"

"Get out of the way and maybe I will." When she moved aside I gave my hair a few brushes, went to put on my dress. A simple school dress. I wasn't excited about this visit. Maybe I was afraid Mama would cancel it at the last minute.

At visiting time Bella ran ahead of me to the bench where Mama sat right in the middle. She jumped into her arms. Mama hugged her tight. I stood back and watched.

Mama had on a lavender dress. No more black. And she'd got plump again, like she used to be before she got sick, before Papa died. She still pulled her hair back in a bun, but not tight, so a few curls hung down at the back.

She held out her hand to me. "Celia?"

I walked toward her. Bella slid off her lap and sat at her side. I took Mama's hand in mine, put my other arm around her, fell against her and we hugged and hugged. Tears in her eyes mirrored mine. I could see her black eyes through mine while I wiped my tears.

Bella touched her face. "Mama, are you all well now?"

"Almost. Almost, my darling."

"Can we come home soon?"

"Soon."

"Do you think you'll be well by June?"

"I hope. So what goes on in June?"

"It's the program our class is putting on. The mothers and fathers can come. Can you? Do you think you can?"

"The doctors test me. If I test okay. I come."

I tapped Mama's shoulder. "My class is having a presentation, too. But don't worry, Mama. We want you there, but if you can't come the Home said they'll send someone."

"We don't want anyone else, Celia. Only Mama." Bella stroked Mama's face.

"What about Sammy? Can you bring him?"

"He works hard, still delivers for Western Union. Sells produce with our neighbor."

"What about Blackie? Do they still keep Blackie in their shed?"

"He's safe. You shouldn't worry. On a ranch in San Fernando. They took him to live there. The neighbors bought a truck, you see. They sell more that way,"

I said, "Tell Sammy we miss him. He better answer my last letter!"

"He's not so good at writing. But I'll tell him. To me he should write more, too. So tell me, do they still give you good food? The nutritionists?"

"It's okay," Bella said. "They take us on trips. Did you know? We went to a lake, to a movie, to a restaurant."

"Really? That's wonderful. You enjoy?"

"Mama." I stood up. "I wrote you letters about that. Didn't you get them?"

"Yes, Celia. Now I remember. I had a lot on my mind."

At least she didn't seem to have that melancholia any more. I sat down, patted her knee.

"Mama," Bella said, "Remember how Blackie helped bring our stuff when we moved from our first house her to our new home? I hope he's happy at the ranch."

"Why shouldn't he? Fresh air. Room to run around."

"Mama, remember the horse sheds before we came to California?" I said. "The stables? They were dark inside."

"Of course. The oats, the manure…"

"Mama, Celia, I remember, too. I can remember lots of stuff from New York. Papa used to take us to the delicatessen. Remember?"

I smiled. "Remember the big pickle jar? He held you to reach in and grab one."

"I loved those pickles. You made pickles, too, Mama."

"You want I should teach you the recipe? When we're all together again."

"It's nicer in California, I think. Remember how nice our new house looks when the flowers are in bloom? Are they in bloom now, Mama?"

"I suppose. When we all get back we'll water, we'll take care."

We looked around us. Lots of little buds on the bushes showed signs of wanting to open wide. The gardeners would make sure we had plenty of flowers on the grounds in summer.

We saw family groups stirring, leaving, marching down the paths. It was so sad that it was time for us to go now, too. Lots of hugging and kissing before we left Mama at the gate.

At supper Rachel-Ann sat next to me. She looked not at me, but down into her bowl of chicken soup with its chunks of white meat and strings of noodles, and said,

"Me and Leonard didn't have any visitors today. So we went into the garden together."

Was I supposed to be jealous or something? I didn't care. I said, "That's nice."

"We tied up tomato plants together."

"You should have lots of ripe tomatoes coming up."

It didn't rain in January. But when February came it poured. I tried on my raincoat. It didn't fit. I was going to give it to Bella, but the material was cracked and the edges worn away. Hers was falling apart, too. We couldn't even give them to the smaller children. We had to throw them away.

We wore our cloth coats to school and back. If they got wet we rested them on the radiators at school until they dried. It was cozy in our classrooms. I did my work and Helen did hers beside me. Still, there was a restless feeling that couldn't leave me. It was a nameless worry. I stole glances at Helen, so industrious and serious today. That was calming. That and the warmth from the radiators.

In April Helen asked me if I wanted to hunt Easter eggs with her at her house. No, I didn't want to. But I liked helping decorate the classroom with cut-outs of eggs that we decorated with our colored pencils. Green, purple, and yellow zigzags. And we also drew Easter bunnies. When my picture was done, I held it up for Helen to see, took a deep breath, and said,

"I have to stay home tomorrow, Helen, and help get ready for Passover."

"Another Jewish Holiday? How many do you-all have, anyway?"

"More than you know. Our Hebrew calendar shows different ones all the time. Passover is the holiest."

"How come?"

Passover celebrates our flight from Egypt when the Red Sea parted to let us escape from the pharaoh."

"I know that story." Helen rocked back on her chair.

I pushed her forward, her feet landed flat under her desk. "Be careful. And did you know that we can't eat bread in Passover week? We have to eat unleavened bread."

"What's that?"

"It's called 'matzos'. I'll show you. I have some in my lunch. But don't eat it. You won't like it. Maybe you will. I don't know." I shrugged my shoulders.

Helen pushed her chair back again. "Let me try."

I looked around the room. All the kids were busy writing in their spelling workbooks. I reached inside the compartment under my desk, opened my lunch bag with one hand, reached inside with the other. I felt for a piece of Matzos, broke off a jagged little square. "Here. Try this."

She put it in her mouth, chewed. "It's kind of dry."

The teacher stared at us. I wrote some words in my workbook, waited, then whispered to Helen, "It's good with butter."

That was how Papa used to give it to us. I wasn't sure if that was kosher or not. The Home seemed to have different rules for eating than we had with my parents.

At recess Helen and I could talk on our way to play dodge ball with our teams.

"Why do they make such dry bread?"

"It's when they crossed the Red Sea. They only had flour and water and no yeast. So they mixed the dough like that, shaped it flat like pancakes, and they put the cakes on their heads when they walked across so the sun could bake it as they went."

"On their heads? That's funny."

"I know. But that's the way they told me the story. It is funny." We giggled. "But it worked. It baked."

Our team won, which felt good, put me in a happy mood. When we got back to our seats I leaned back in my chair like she'd done.

This time she pushed me forward. "What else do you eat with your matzos?"

"We got to drink wine on Passover back home. Here we have grape juice, and we have special food, like hard-boiled eggs, parsley, lamb, because they have special meanings."

"At Easter we have special things, too. Ham. Besides wine and wafers at Mass."

'We couldn't talk any longer because the teacher had us begin rehearsals for the end-of-the-year program then.

We got good news in the first week of May. Mama was coming to visit us again. She was almost well. Bella and I looked at each other and grinned. We probably seemed like happy idiots.

We met Mama on the bench, as usual, hugged and sat.

Bella said, "How are Uncle and Tante? And Isaac? Do they write to you? And did you tell Sammy we missed him?"

"All well, all are well, *Gottsadank.*"

"Mama, do the doctors think you'll be all right?" I said.

"Very soon, darlings. Very soon."

Bella piped up. "Do you want to hear my poem, Mama? I'll rehearse it for the recitation in June."

She stood straight and tall in front of us. Mama and I held hands, sat on the bench side by side to watch her. The sun felt warm, the first flowers of spring lined the path up to the main building. Pink and violet petals rose up among the green.

Bella said "Ahem.". She clasped her hands in front of her, opened her mouth.

"Wait, "I called out. "Look." I pointed to the path.

Mrs. Mack seemed to tip side to side as she walked, fast as her stout legs could go, right in our direction. She stopped, out of breath.

"Mrs. Heuer, Dr. Frey needs to talk to you."

Mama stood up. "The children?"

"Yes, the children, too."

Mrs. Mack hugged Bella, then reached to the other side of Mama to hug me, too. She motioned for us to go on. She stayed by the bench, catching her breath.

Dr. Frey didn't send Ethel, I noticed. This must be more important. It was scary. I didn't look to the left or right so I could not see other family groups out on the lawn. So they wouldn't see us, either, I hoped. Silly me.

Our shoes clip-clopped across the marble floor of the large hall. We found Dr. Frey's door shut. Mama and I stood there, hesitated. Bella lifted her hand, rapped her knuckles on the wood.

"Come."

Dr. Frey motioned for Mama to sit in the large chair across from his desk, and for us to sit in chairs against the wall behind her.

Mama leaned forward. "Good afternoon. I hope you are well this day."

"Yes, fine thank you, Mrs. Heuer. Or should I say Mrs. Raphael."

He picked up a newspaper clipping from the desk, held it out to her.

"Oh."

He studied me and Bella sitting there, our mouths shut tight, eyes straight ahead.

"You didn't tell your *kinderlach*? The children don't know?"

"I...I wanted to wait until their school year was finished. They should finish their year."

"No no no." He hit the desk with his hand. "It doesn't work that way. We need space for more orphans. We know of many other children in need. They need the places your girls can give them. It would be a *mitzvah*. A good deed. Take them home. Make room."

"Yes, I was going to."

I whispered, "Can I see that paper?"

He handed it to me.

> RIVERSIDE COUNTY, CALIFORNIA
> Vital Statistics
> Announcements
> Mrs. Esther Heuer married to Mr. Harry Raphael.

Bella reached across, snatched it out of my hands even as I sat on the edge of my chair studying the fragile paper.

She glanced at it. "Mama, did you get married?" she asked.

Our mother turned her chair around, reached out her arms to us. "Yes, I wanted to tell you. To Mr. Raphael. You remember him? He was Papa's friend. They both sold produce. Remember him?"

"Isn't he Julius' father? And Abraham's?"

She nodded, tears in her eyes.

Dr. Frey stood up. "Mr. Raphael is living at your home now? and you are home now? You must take your daughters home."

"Yes, yes." She wiped her eyes. "Shouldn't they stay first for their school term to finish?"

"We have a waiting list. They are good girls. They will be fine. Your health is better. The girls will have a step-father." He called for the gardener.

"Find their suitcases in the storage shed," he told the gardener. "We always keep our children's valises that they came with. The tags say Heuer. Did you have more than one apiece? No? Bring them to the girls' cottage."

"Will we stay for supper, Dr. Frey?" Bella asked. The clock on the wall said it was almost that time.

"Your mother will provide. She should have told me herself. I had to read it in a journal. Your car is here, no?"

"You didn't come on the streetcar, Mama?"

"No, my babies. Mr. Raphael drove me. He's in the car out in front. He waits."

Back in our cottage, Mama sat on my bed. I'd smoothed it real tight that morning. Her body made wrinkles where she sat. She put her head in her hands.

When the suitcases came, we dusted them off, opened them up.

Mrs. Mack pushed our door open, stepped inside our room. She cried. Hugged us. "I told him he should wait. He said he couldn't. Too many orphans. Need beds. Let me help you, girls. No, sit, Mrs. Heuer. You relax."

I folded all my clothes as precisely as I could. Bella folded hers, too, but not so neatly. Mrs. Mack opened all our drawers and closets. Then we got our hairbrushes, toothbrushes, the knickknacks we'd collected.

"Can I say goodbye to my friends?" Bella asked her. She nodded. Bella walked out the door. "I'll be right back."

I knew Rachel-Ann would be with her father, a rare visit. He worked far away. But today of all days he came. I would not take her precious time with him away to say goodbye. Besides, I didn't want to cry in front of Mama.

Alice came in and hugged me. "You were my helper, Celia. You don't even know how much you helped, talking to the little ones, explaining to them, being so kind."

"You're the kind one, Alice." I was still in awe of her. I'd grown, but she was still taller. She smiled, winked at me, said, "Good luck."

She helped me carry my suitcase. Mama took Bella's. We found Bella at the gate with three girls. They saw us approach, the girls scattered. I looked around to see if Leonard or any of the boys I knew were nearby. They weren't. On Sundays with no visitors they stayed in the back by the woodshop and gardens.

We saw Mr. Raphael's dusty, white car with a rounded top and a black running board parked on the street, just outside the gate. He got out, raised his eyebrows at us, then said he was happy to see us. He helped us in, drove off with Mama in the front seat beside him, Bella and me in the back.

We were on our way home. Why I did not feel happy, I did not know.

Chapter 16

Home on Thirty-Third Street Home Sweet Home

On the trip home I stared out the window. Bella kept quieter than ever before.

What a silent car ride. Where was all the background noise I was used to hearing? Girls chattering, dishes clattering, clothes rustling, plus car motors and honking from outside on the streets. Not in this quiet car.

Mr. Raphael tried to get us to talk but I refused to say anything.

"I didn't expect to drive you home today." He kept his eyes on the road ahead but talked directly to us in the seat behind him. "But I'm very glad to have you come back with us."

Who expected this? Mama didn't. We didn't.

"You will make your mama happy."

"Yes, yes." Mama turned around to look at us, wiped her eyes.

The scenery, familiar in some places, strange in others, did not match how I felt. Somehow my outlook wasn't bright, not like the red, pink and white oleander flowers that lined front yards. Or the light yellow-tinged fronds of the palm trees that stood out in the fading sunlight.

The sights turned dismal and matched the uneasy way I felt when we came to bleak factories, gray houses and drainage pipes along dirt highways that I looked at through the car windows

We turned and crossed four rows of train tracks. This was familiar. I watched the long metal rails in their gravel beds stretch out in the distance. We turned south on Central Avenue, drove on down to 33rd Street. Our block looked different now, our house smaller, cars parked along the curbs made the street look narrow. Maybe I looked different to Mama, too.

Mr. Raphael parked in the roadway beside our house where we used to lead Blackie to his shed. I noticed that Bella craned her head to see the back. She'd miss Blackie more than anyone. Mama hustled out of the car. She turned to us.

"I'm running inside, I'll make sure everything is good for you." She clambered up the porch stairs so fast.

"Stay." Mr. Raphael turned to the back seat, looked at me and Bella. His light brown hair, parted on the side, combed nice, made his forehead and cheeks look smooth to match. His head was round, his ears stuck out to the sides, kind of funny looking. He wore a light tan suit and brown necktie.

"You are good girls, I know. You should be happy your mother is better at last. I helped take care of her you should know. She needed me. She is happy after so much tragedy. Are you glad for her?"

I shrugged. Bella stared out the window.

"I had sadness, too, you should know. Maybe you knew her? My children's mother, Rose?"

I shook my head.

"She was a friend with your mother. Cancer she had."

I hugged myself. Ugly word. I never heard it before but the way he said it, such a terrible sounding illness.

"Let's go in. Please tell your mother everything's all right. She'll never smile again if her girls aren't happy. She asks for you every day. You should know."

"Okay," I walked ahead.

Inside, I saw Mama in the kitchen next to a redheaded, bushy-haired young lady stirring a pot. This lady dropped her spoon, ran toward us, knelt down.

"So you are Bella and Celia. Everyone wanted you to come back."

Who was this? She called Mr. Raphael Dad.

"This is Blossom." Mama came over now. She put her arms around Bella and me. "These are my little ones. Blossom is Harry's oldest child. She's staying with us for now."

Blossom set the table and said there was enough soup for us all.

Her soup didn't taste as good as the Home's. Blossom must have made it herself, because Mama's would never taste this bland.

"Harry, bring in the girls' suitcases," Mama said.

He'd already brought them in. When we looked at our old room, what a shock. Blossom took over one of the beds, covered it with a lacy spread. She placed her cosmetics and glass bottles all over the dresser.

Mama stood in the doorway, wrung her hands.

"Girls, you can sleep in one bed tonight, like you used to when you were very little. Do you remember?"

We nodded, went right to bed early, woke up a half hour later.

"Celia! Bella!" Sam shook my shoulders. Bella's too. He sat on our bed. "Wake up."

That's all it took. Dark outside now, but we were wide awake.

"Didn't Mama tell you to wait up for me?" Get up. Come to the table. She makes me supper every night now that she's home. Come sit with us." Sam wore his messenger uniform, a leather sash from his shoulder to his waist. How tall he got, and handsome. He motioned for us to follow him out the door.

Wearing our nightgowns, we joined him at the table. Blossom and Mr. Raphael sat there, picked at their desserts with their forks. Mama gave us tea in her best teacups. She gave us more of the beef stew she served Sam, and pieces of apple cake. Now everyone talked at once. Except Bella, who mostly peered beneath lowered eyelids at Mama and at Mr. Raphael and at Sam.

"School, Mama," said Sam. "They have to be enrolled."

I said, "There's less than a month left. Maybe we better stay home till September."

"No." Harry pounded the table. "Education. The girls need to finish, and my boys will when they come back."

That was the first I heard that Julius and Abraham were coming, too.

Mama said, "Harry, go sleep in the boys' room tonight. The room with Sam. I'd like my girls with me."

"But I'm your husband..." He stopped, smiled. "Of course. You need to be with them."

After we did the dishes we climbed into Mama's bed on either side of her. She hugged us, stroked my hair.

"You know something, *Maidlach*?"

"What, Mama?' Bella snuggled closer in her arms.

"You've both grown so much. At first I was afraid."

"Of what?" I turned my head to look into her eyes.

"That maybe you weren't my same daughters." She laughed, a silly sounding noise it seemed to me.

"Of course we're the same." I didn't like it when she talked like that.

"*Sha sha*, my little girls. Have nice dreams."

Her soft, feather-filled quilt felt familiar, warm and cozy. Bella fell asleep right away. Mama did, too, one of her arms around me, but I shrugged it off.

First I stared at the wall, then at the ceiling. Both showed bulky shadows that moved slowly about the way my thoughts did. I couldn't see out the window but I remembered how it used to look outside. Probably it would look different now.

I turned my pillow around to the cold side. Huntington Park wouldn't have changed. I could figure out which streets to travel on to go back there. I had money for carfare now, too. Sam had slipped me some coins. I would wait till the last day of school. The teacher would think I'd been sick or something and she'd let me back in with my class. I'd say my poem and then stay on the playground and talk with my friends.

When I finally fell asleep I didn't dream. I woke up in the morning able to look at my thoughts in the light of day. It wouldn't work to go back. What a stupid thought.

I tried to be cheerful around Mama like Bella was. The three of us slept together for the next few nights. Then Harry brought in a cot for Blossom, so Bella and I got our own beds again.

I brushed my hair in the morning to get ready for school. Blossom came up behind me, looked in the mirror, blotted her orange lip rouge.

"Celia, I'm going to Australia. As soon as I save up enough money. I'm excited about going."

"Australia? That's so far away."

"I know. I have relatives there. They wrote Dad that I could come stay with them." She sloshed on perfume. The hazy scent followed her out the door.

Bella and I had attended Wadsworth Avenue School before, but when we enrolled now we felt like new kids. At recess Bella ran to my classroom. I walked with her to a bench by the edge of the playground. She stood, stared at the street beyond our chain link fence.

"Oh, Sweetie, doesn't school not seem the way you remember?" I took her hand in mine.

"No. I liked our Miles Avenue School near the Home better."

"Yeah, I know what you mean. Huntington Park is far away. We should try to make friends here."

"What about your old friends, Celia?"

"I'm not in the same class with them. They put me in the graduating class, getting ready for high school. Oh, Bella. The kids know all their songs and they've rehearsed and everything. I got mixed up and one girl laughed at me."

She understood. I could never tell this to Mama. So good to have a sister.

A ball got away from a boy who played kickball on the macadam not far from us. Bella kicked the ball back to him. She always was really good at sports.

"What about you, Bella?"

"The work's too easy. "The teacher said my work was fine."

"Have you run into your old friend Gracie?"

"She's not in my class. But I saw her. She has her own friends now. She runs with a fast crowd."

"Little Gracie?"

"Yep."

"How do you know that?"

"I heard some girl say so."

I smiled. I don't think Bella had any idea what that meant. Maybe later she'd give Gracie a chance to be friends. But only if Gracie was nice like she used to be.

On the way back to my classroom I tried to look for anything that had not changed since I went away. The steel monkey bars were still in place. But the kids jumping down from them seemed awfully little.

When the bell rang at the end of school Bella found me again. We walked home together along streets that should have looked familiar. The branches on trees above our heads held avocados and lemons like before. I had to duck when we came to a sparsely-leaved loquat tree, loaded with little yellow fruits that hung low over the sidewalk. I wondered if this was the tree where Abraham picked the loquats he thought gave him appendicitis. But I didn't mention this to Bella.

We walked up the steps to our front door together, onto the porch we'd played on so often when we were younger. Bella said, "Do your homework real slow, Celia."

"Why?"

"So we'll need to wait for supper till Sam gets off work, and we'll get to eat with him."

"Good thinking, Bella." The screen door slammed behind us.

Mama had a new piece of furniture. A black Victrola on curvy legs stood next to her easy chair against the wall. I wanted so much to touch it, put on records, tap my feet, listen to songs. I wasn't sure if music was what Mama wanted right now. To please her I sat with her. I didn't ask, but picked up my handiwork.

Bella and I showed Mama the embroidery stitches we'd learned at the Home. She kept a basket at her feet with worked-on knitting, crocheting, tatting–a lot of scarves and sweaters she'd started but never finished. Instead, Mama darned socks.

Bella picked up the tatting shuttle. "This is so smooth, like the darning egg. I like to feel the outside." She ran her fingers up and down the edge.

"That's not what it's for. Use it like Mama showed us. Here's some thread." I threw a spool at her.

She threw it back at me.

"Girls. Be nice. Listen. Today I got a letter from Tante Becky and Uncle."

"How are they?" I wasn't sure I cared. I loved them but was still mad that they left when Mama needed them.

"Lots of news. Isaac wants to quit school and work on the produce truck full time. Cousin Theodore joined the army, he's going to fight in France. They're all worried about him."

Bella said, "President Wilson said it's our duty. We have to fight against Germany."

"Such a terrible thing, war."

We worked with our yarn, let the noise from the street cover our silence.

"Theo's going to send us all letters. And souvenirs for the girls, he said. Little American flags on sticks he told Tante."

After a few minutes Bella said, "Celia, have you written any letters? To Helen? To Rachel-Ann?"

"Not yet. How about you?"

"Not yet."

The front door opened. A banging slam. Every evening when Blossom finished work she came right home.

"Look what I brought everybody!" She set her packages on the little table by the sofa.

"From Woolworth's."

She worked behind the cosmetic counter. She opened some bags and pulled out little dangling gold earrings. She set one pair with red stones in front of Bella, another with small blue stones she put on my lap.

"Mama pieced our ears when we were babies" I said. "The holes grew together, though." I narrowed my eyes. Maybe Mama wouldn't want me to tell that. Too bad. I didn't care.

Mama held up her hand. "That was the style then. Now not. Now my girls are too young for the style these days. Now is different."

"Oh, I didn't know." Blossom waved her hands in the air. "Wrap them up again. Keep them till you're older and you can reopen your ears. Listen." The back door slammed. "Here comes Dad."

Mr. Raphael came in through the kitchen. He sat down in a straight-backed chair with a green tapestry cushion, closed his eyes for a moment, caught his breath, and said,

"I pick up the boys from the train on Saturday. "Who wants to go to the station with me?"

"Not me." I didn't have to explain why.

"Mr. Raphael," Bella said, "We don't like that train station."

"Fine, fine. But you don't have to keep calling me Mr. Raphael. At least try Harry. I'm your stepfather. Bella, Celia. Don't ever think..." He got up from his chair to stand in front of the two of us. "You know I'll never take the place of your father. I knew Louis. He was my friend. I'll never be Louis. But at least let me be as good a stepfather as I can. No more of this Mr. Raphael stuff."

"All right, Harry." I said. When he told us Papa was his friend I decided I could like him. I would call him whatever he wanted. Not what Mama wanted. What he himself thought best. I nodded. Yes. It was my decision.

Mama set down her crocheting. She went to Bella. "You don't have to do that. You can call him what you want. Maybe later you'll change."

I shook my head, kept on stabbing my needle in and out through a round of beige cloth.

Mama said," Come, dinner's ready. Sammy will be late tonight. Has to deliver the late shift telegrams again."

So we ate early after all. After supper we went back to sit in the front room again. Blossom gently set a shiny black record on its round bed in the Victrola. She lifted the metal arm and made sure its needle fit the first groove. The music started out low. We picked up our embroidery, and suddenly heard a loud scream—a scream of pain from Bella.

She had sat down on a crochet hook. The metal point had stuck straight into her thigh.

We tripped over ourselves in our rush to help her. First Mama tried to pull it out. Bella screamed louder. "Don't touch it. Help!"

I tried, she pushed me away.

"Let me see if I can get it." Blossom lifted Bella's skirt, grabbed the handle, and Bella screamed bloody murder. She pushed Blossom away, held the handle against her leg and ran around in circles.

"Now, now. Let me." Harry picked her up and laid her on the sofa on her side. He made sure her skirt was away from the hook, but covering her underwear for modesty. "Wait. Calm down. There, there."

Bella's screams became sobs and groans.

Harry knelt beside her on the sofa. He looked closely at her wound, felt around it.

"No, we can't pull it. The hook is to the back. We can't twist it, either. It needs…" He held it in the place where it had entered her flesh. Gently, he manipulated it until the point of the hook was deeper than at the skin. One, two, three, he angled it just right, then pulled it out.

Bella gave out a short cry, then sobbed. Mama ran to get cotton and Mercurochrome. She cleaned the wound and bandaged Bella's thigh while the rest of us stood around feeling useless.

"Bella. See if you can take a few steps." Harry took her hand, helped her off the couch.

"Yes. I think I can. It doesn't hurt any more. It feels all right now." She touched the bandage.

"Yes, I can step, I can dance." Bella twirled. She looked over her shoulder at Harry and said, "Thanks, Dad."

The rest of us, Mama, especially, gave out sighs of relief, went back to our handiwork.

Mr. Raphael, Harry, no, Dad, smiled so much, the skin next to his eyes crinkled at the edges. He sat back, clasped his hands to his chest, nodded, the smile never left his mouth.

The record finished and the needle scratched back and forth over the middle part of the disk that didn't have any grooves for music on it. Blossom came to the rescue and put on a new record.

This song's name was "And they called it Dixieland." Happy music. Blossom knew the words and sang out, "They called it Twice as Nice as Paradise."

Sam walked in, saw us all bouncing to the music, hugged Mama.

I could see how happy Mama looked after all the sadness she'd been through. I wondered if that feeling would last. I touched my hand to my forehead, pushed back a whisp of hair, nodded in time to the music.

On Saturday Dad picked up Julius and Ray at the station. I say Ray because Abraham had changed his name while he was away. No more Abe.

Bella was not shy with them. "You'll be going to my school," she told Julius. "Ray and Celia will go on to Jefferson High School."

"But we won't be in the same grades," I was quick to point out.

Bella lifted up her hand. "Look. We're none of us the same. I'm the youngest, then comes Julius, then Celia, then Ray. Ray, you're the oldest. Except for Sam. He doesn't want to go to school any more. Did you go to school where you stayed before?"

Ray nodded. His little brother Julius said, "It's better here. Your mother makes good potato pancakes."

That was the last good thing I heard him say about Mama. Especially after the fifty cents. That happened later.

Dad put his boys to work at the produce stand. Julius and Ray already knew how to weigh and pack and clean the vegetables so they'd look good to sell. They knew how to display the fruit, clean up the trimmings. They knew how to make change when customers paid.

But Mama saw that Julius always used to sneak out fifty cents that should have gone in the change drawer. And finally she told Dad.

"I don't need your old fifty cents," I heard him yell at Dad. "Or *any* money. I get in the movies free. I just walk in. At the Million Dollar Theater they don't even see me. And I only need a penny for the streetcar." He threw some coins down on the floor and walked out the door.

Dad lifted his arm up, ran out after him, like he wanted to hit him. But Mama pulled him back.

"It's okay, Harry. He's just a boy."

"But I can't let the children steal."

Mama face tightened. She opened her mouth to say something, thought better of it, walked into the kitchen.

Julius should have got paid for working. If he was paid he wouldn't have to take any coins. I believed that, and I wanted to tell that to Mama. And tell his father, too. But instead I walked outside. The sidewalk shone in the moonlight. I saw bunches of stars up above, though I couldn't remember their names from science class. Maybe Leonard would know. But I would never see him again. I walked to the corner.

I had money in my pocket. What Sam gave me along with whatever I'd saved up.

I walked to the corner, looked down the block to see if a streetcar came this time of night. Yes, one passed by and I knew another would follow. If I got on, I could transfer to the bus to Huntington Park. I thought again about going back, finishing school there. Again I knew it was not a good idea. Then I remembered that when I was at the Home I longed to come back here where I am now. I scratched my head, stared down at the sidewalk.

I wished Mama would try harder to get my stepbrother to like her. Make him more potato pancakes or cookies or something.

Branches of trees behind the street light waved in a light breeze, made shadows on the front of a wooden office building at the corner. Traffic noise sounded like a steady murmur. I had on a new dress Mama bought for me in a shop on Broadway. The short sleeves covered my shoulders in a modern style that left my arms bare. The night air felt warm on my arms and face.

What would next semester be like, with all of us living in the house?

I turned back toward home, saw Ray come toward me. He walked fast, didn't seem to want to stop to talk to me. I stood in his way so he'd have to.

"What's happening at the house?" I said.

"Same thing. Dad's lecturing Julius. I didn't want to listen."

"How come you changed your name?"

"Abraham is too old fashioned."

"I'm really glad you did. Mama is, too."

"Why? Because of your brother who died?"

"Sure. Every time Abraham's name comes up she cries."

Ray leaned toward me, stuck his hands in his pockets. "That's pretty sad."

"I know. Where're you going?"

"To a friend's house. They let me drive their car."

"You're only thirteen years old!"

"Don't you think I know that? Dad said he'd teach me to drive the produce truck soon, too. And I'm going to be fourteen soon, besides."

"Oh boy." I stepped to the side to let him go on his way but he stayed, happy to talk about his favorite things, cars.

"And I get to work on the brakes. I'm gonna be a mechanic, you know. That's what I'll study"

"Julius likes cars, too."

"Dad's gonna let him drive. And he can work on the engine with me when I get to take it apart and stuff."

"Really? Don't you guys want to do college or stuff? Like me?"

"You?"

I nodded. "Do you want to know what I'm going to study in high school?"

"What?" He scuffed his shoe at the ground, looked back the way he was headed.

"Journalism. I want to be a newspaper reporter."

"Yeah, I suppose girls can do that. See you later."

I watched him walk, saw that he still wore his knickers and long stockings, even though I knew that they bought him long pants to wear when high school started.

I felt like walking farther, because outside the warm evening helped me feel free. I passed the new high school they'd built while I was away. The builders modeled it after Thomas Jefferson's home Monticello, so they called the school Jefferson High School. Bella would get to go to a new kind of a school, a junior high.

I recognized more of the houses I used to walk by when I was younger. I wasn't ready to go home yet. I remembered that I heard Mama cough while Dad gave Julius a talking-to. Dad said earlier that if everyone was well, we'd go to the beach on Sunday, to the Venice canals where he knew a special place to park the truck. If she was well.

When Bella and I first came back from the Home and we slept

in Mama's room I'd noticed a big envelope with the name of the sanitarium. Yellow and thick, it rested on the opened roll top desk that used to belong to Papa. Scrawled on it in heavy black ink read the title: Health Report for Esther Heuer. The envelope looked scary, and I knew I wasn't supposed to touch it.

Suddenly I wanted to know what it said inside. Not to see if she'd be well enough to go to the beach, but if she'd ever get all the way better.

I had to know. I had to get back home. Now. I turned and ran. Fast down the block, nearly tripping on a place where the sidewalk had cracks.

I ran up the steps into the front room. Dad in his chair, read the newspaper. He called out to me, "We have grapes on the table. Take some."

"Thanks." I glanced at them, black and shiny, but with seeds, I knew, and ran into the kitchen. Mama was rolling out dough to make *lokshen* noodles. Bella sat at the table, her schoolbooks spread in front of her,

"Wanna check my work, Celia?"

"Later."

I peeked in at the boy's room. Julius was lost in a library book, didn't see me.

No one saw me tiptoe into Mama's room. I made straight for the desk. I could see the edges of the manila envelope underneath a bunch of papers, stacked in a messy sort of way, jumbled up. The letterhead on the top paper told that this paper came from a bank.

I forced my mind to stop racing. I sat in Mama's chair, read this letter and went through all those receipts and other papers. Loans coming due, even a nice note from Uncle Isaac, letting her pay back later. Mama had no money, was poor while we were gone. Poorer than I ever gave a thought to. I understood about the fifty cents. You could buy a loaf of bread, a dozen eggs and a quart of milk with those fifty cents. Of course she wouldn't let me and Bella know about being poor. Of course I could see now that the Orphan's Home was for poor orphans and poor half orphans. Mama didn't want us to know that when Papa died we got poor. Sam knew. That was why he worked. Of course.

I leaned back in the chair and took a deep breath. I didn't even try to put the papers back in the order I'd found them, didn't care if Mama knew that I knew.

I said out loud, "I think I'm old enough to help her. I think I can take care of her better than she can take care of me. At least I can help with her paperwork. Ha. Now let's see about her coughing."

I opened the large yellow envelope. Lots of papers here, too. Test results in medical language. Diagnosis, Prognosis, Tuberculosis. All those Osis's. I understood them pretty much. They added up to that she was safe to go home, but would need tests from time to time.

Up in a cubby hole in the top part of the desk I saw familiar stamps on a stack of envelopes. Those were the letters I'd sent from the Home. I took the top one out, peeled the pages out from the thin envelope, read:

"Dear Mama. I am glad you will be coming to our end-of-the-year program. They chose me to say a poem. I practice it in front of the mirror so I won't make any mistakes. I only have two more tests to take. If I get good grades on them, I will get a good grade in the class. That will make it good when I go to high school because then they will see I get good grades and put me in high classes. I will get a diploma and you will be able to be so proud of me."

What a stupid letter. It sounded so babyish. I could write a better letter than that. How much better it would have been if I never told her that I was glad she would come to our program.

I stuffed the stationery into the envelope in time to look behind me and see Mama watching me from the doorway.

"You kept my letters, Mama."

"They're from my little girl. Why should I not keep?" She took the envelope from my hands, kissed it, sat down on my bed, and cried.

"Celia, I read the letters. Yours, Bella's. She said she gets an honor too. My girls are so smart." Between sobs she said, "Everyone—Sam, Harry, the neighbors, they all said you should stay, get your honors. You worked so hard. How could I take you away? But I wanted my girls with me. So bad."

Another sob. "They said no. Let them stay. A few more weeks, you can fix up their room, get them good beds, they're not little any more. Fix their closets. Be ready. The minute they get diplomas, then take them. The very minute."

I listened, nodded, but I didn't cry.

"What could I do?" She wiped one eye with the corner of her apron.

"What about Blossom?" I said.

"She's his daughter. She left her boarding house. She asked could she stay while she gets ready. What could I say? No? So far away she's going. To their family in another country."

"I know. Australia. She told me." I put my arms around Mama. She let me hug her. Her hair smelled like peaches

"Remember when you made us peaches with cream for breakfast, Mama?"

"I do, my Celinka. We did in summer. I can make it again. Would you like that?"

A sudden flood of tears down my cheeks surprised me. It was the memory of all our past breakfasts in New York, in our first house here, and everywhere, when we were a happy family. Mama's eyes filled with water, too. I laid my check against hers. So soft. I reached out my hand to hold hers. Her fingers clasped mine tightly. We sat together for a long time. Music came from the front room.

"Someone put a record on the Victrola," I said

She wiped her eyes, stood up. "We'll listen. We'll be all right."

For a while all of us sat on cushioned chairs in the front room listening to the up and down notes of a lilting Viennese waltz. Even Julius came in for a while. He carried his book, and read it while listening. Bella took her books back into our bedroom, and came in to listen. Mama tiptoed back into the kitchen to boil water for her noodles.

I stepped out onto the front porch. The music sounded full, but faint. The night air still felt warm. Breezes swept past my face, lifted the ends of my hair. The perfume from the jasmine bush at the neighbor's house gave off a prettier scent than our new shampoo had made my hair smell.

The door slammed. Now who?

Bella came to me, leaned her shoulder against mine. She asked me a funny question.

"Celia, do you think if Papa was still alive he would want us not to call him Papa anymore? But to call him Dad like the American kids?"

"No. I do not. He was Papa to us and to Mama. He would stay Papa to us as long as he lived."

Bella skipped a few steps, kissed me on the forehead, and ran back into the house.

This was my home. Even in the dark I could see the fruit trees and the palm trees outlined against the dim sky. This was California, the place Papa had brought us to.

Sam and Bella and I were still young. Our lives would be here.

I loved waking up in the mornings, looking out the window to smile at the mountains above the tall buildings downtown. These were the very same mountains I saw when we lived in the Jewish Orphans' home. In winter their tops, so white where snow had fallen, glistened in the sun. Imagine. Snow in California. In summer the whole range stood out with a purple luster.

I felt glad that Papa got to see the mountains, too, before he died. He even took us to the beach to see the ocean, and said it was calmer than the one he crossed over to come to America.

I twirled around in a circle here on my front porch. I breathed in the clear air and sniffed the new blossoms on the orange and lemon trees around us.

Los Angeles was surrounded by mountains. I felt protected in this circle of hills. Papa was right. This home would be good for us.

END

Blackie, the white horse

The family before Papa died

Barbara Rowland Lubick was born in Los Angeles, has lived in Tujunga and Sherman Oaks, and is a graduate of UCLA. She is interested in sculpting the human figure in clay. She has been a junior high school teacher and a middle school counselor and has a master's degree in counseling. She lives in Winnetka, California, is married, and has three children and four grandchildren.

Made in the USA
San Bernardino, CA
09 October 2015